I0580781

MAGNOLIA

REAWAKENED

LIV EVANS

ZAC PILOT

Magnolia
First published by Liv Evans and Zac Pilot in April 2024
as part of the Ever After? Anthology.
Current/expanded version published in June 2024.
ISBN 9781763514928
© 2024 by Liv Evans and Zac Pilot

For any enquiries please visit www.livevans.com.au

Cover design: Liv Evans

Editing: Marni M (@mmacrae on Fiverr)

Illustrations: Claudio S (@iaioart on Fiverr)

For those fighting for what matters.

CHAPTER
ONE

"*Missiles locked and loaded.*"

Magnolia "Mags" Hua announced as she locked her missile on her target. The simulator console vibrated beneath her as the crosshairs settled right over the slick armoured carapace of the alien Hundun.

"*I'm covering your six,*" Willow chimed in through the comms. "*We have two ships coming in from your seven o'clock. I've got eyes on them. You keep following the others.*"

"*Gladly.*" Mags observed the way the naturally armoured plates overlapped, and the stretch of its double pair of membranous leather wings made her stomach churn. It reminded her of a mix between the bats and cockroaches her Earth Studies teacher showed her as a child.

She fired her weapons.

A missile blasted from the launcher on her bird-shaped craft and through the foggy atmosphere, rocketing toward the beast and hitting it in a spectacular display of fire and sparks. The Hun's leather wing started to sizzle away, the creature letting out a low, resonant yowl.

Without hesitation, Mags shot a second missile. It hit the alien beast right in the sweet spot. A shower of gore bloomed across her windscreen, and she grunted as she banked her own plane right to try and avoid the debris.

"Watch out! One of the ships is—"

Mags yelped, pulling to the side hard as her evasive move put her right in the path of an alien Willow was tracking. She tried to avoid it, but she was too slow, and the creature shooting toward her had a death wish.

"Mags!" Willow cried in warning as Mags peered at the alien and prepared to meet her doom—

"Alert! All males aged eighteen and over are required to report to the meeting deck immediately. Alert!"

The simulator whined mechanically as it powered down. The interface helmet Mags wore went black, so she tore it off and slumped back in the seat, placing a hand on her chest as her heart hammered beneath it so hard it hurt.

Red lights pulsed on and off in her living room, and all peripheral electronics around her faded to emergency reserves.

"Alert! All males aged eighteen and over are required to report to the meeting deck immediately. Alert!"

Catching her breath, Mags slid off the seat and staggered from the small, cluttered living room into her bedroom. It had a bunk bed in it and two wardrobes set on either side of a desk. The bottom bunk was stuffed with a pair of threadbare blankets, two pillows, and the pyjamas her siblings had discarded that morning. She ignored the fact that the twins hadn't made their bed, yet again, and climbed the ladder to her bunk, where she shoved her hands under the mattress and pulled out a back-up communicator. She plugged it into the charging socket in her headboard and opened a chat window with Willow.

Hey, you around?

Mags bit her lip and wiped a sheen of sweat off her forehead as the blasted alert hollered through her room. She hoped Willow hadn't left her communicator out in the open again. Last time she had, and her parents had been so scared that she had the contraband tech that they threw it in the trash cycle. Luckily, they'd been too scared to run it outside of their allotted time, so Willow was able to retrieve the device.

I should be asking you that. That was a close call! If that alert hadn't shut the sim down, you would have been in for a nasty hit!

"Don't I know it," Mags grumbled under her breath. She sighed and collapsed against her bed.

Mags had recently decided to take advantage of her father's old training simulator while he and her mother were out for work and her siblings were at school. Her grandmother was asleep in a bunk in her parents' room, but lately she had been sleeping deeper than space. Mags had always hated the stupid rule that only men were able to fight.

Well, I got out before it initiated, so I'm fine. Any chance you can get us eyes on the meeting deck?

Rolling over onto her back, Mags blew dishevelled strands of hair off her face. Her hair was another thing she had always hated, envying how the boys and men got to cut theirs short. Not that she wanted it that close-cropped, but something shorter than the regulated minimum of fifteen centimetres below the chin would be cooler and easier to maintain.

I thought you'd never ask! I'll work on it now. Can you connect to the wall screen? I'll put up a firewall so they won't know we're there.

A wide grin stretched Mags' lips and she forced herself to sit up. She didn't bother with the ladder, instead jumping straight down to the metal floor, then yanked the communicator from the charge port and ran into the living room. She plugged it into one of the ports beneath the large wall screen her family used to watch the evening news or research different plants or historical stories from Earth.

Her foot bounced impatiently against the deck of its own accord, the rhythmic drumming matching the pace of her still elevated heart rate.

It had been a while since those in charge had called an all-hands meeting. Willow and Mags had snuck into that one, too. Digitally, at least. That had been two days before her sixteenth birthday, which was just over two years ago now.

The wall screen flared to life, showing a little window in the top corner where Mags spotted Willow's smiling face. Her friend's dark brown eyes were bright as she gave Mags a playful salute, her hair also messy from the sim helmet.

"Hey, you," Willow said.

Mags couldn't help but think she looked pretty like that. *"Hey."*

Instead of letting her mind wonder what situations they could get into together that would tousle Willow's hair, she returned the unnecessary salute with a lazy one of her own. Then she tore her eyes away from the excitement on Willow's pretty, heart-shaped face and look at the rest of the screen instead.

The meeting deck was the largest empty space on the Worldship Honour. Ever other level was crammed with a mix of living spaces, community rooms, storage, or critical systems such as air purifiers, water generators, engineering spaces, and the like.

With walls barren except for a screen here or there, the wear and tear of humanity's hundred and thirty odd years in space was clear for everyone to see. The scuffs on the floor, however, were covered by the congregation of hundreds of men crammed in together. There was a range of uniform colours represented, from the pieced together grey of engineering overalls, the bronze-trimmed black of slick pilot suits, to the deep green of medical staff.

Mags leaned forward, taking great interest in looking at the proportions of different uniforms. Given that the Empire wanted every single fit and healthy male on flight duty, they made up at least seventy percent of what she saw. Engineering easily made up another fifteen percent. The rest was a hodgepodge of the rare few who were assigned to things like medical, leadership, education, and maintenance.

It took about twenty minutes for the last stragglers to arrive, and just as Mags wondered why there were so many more engineers than she remembered seeing two years ago, a blast door to the rear of the deck opened. The emperor emerged, dressed in a resplendent suit of red trimmed in gold, with his eight cabinet members in white and two guards in black. He was taller than a lot of other men of his generation, his smooth, flawless skin free of the dark bags and stress lines of the pilots or the scars that were hallmarks of the more dangerous positions in engineering or maintenance.

Silence automatically fell over those gathered as the tall man stepped onto a dais at the front of the space. He raised his hand, and the blaring alert finally stopped.

"I guess it's easy to keep your handsome looks when you don't have to lift a finger in your life."

"You think he's handsome? Seriously? You need your damn eyes checked, girl." Mags shook her head. She could count on one hand the number of times she'd ever looked at a man and thought he was handsome. She had hoped Willow was the same but was too scared to bring it up.

Willow and Mags had been born a few weeks apart. Given their close birthdates, they were in the same year at school. They'd known each other since they were five and had been friends ever since Mags punched one of the boys in their year in the face for trying to steal Willow's lunch ration.

"Why? Jealous, Magnolia?"

Mags pressed her lips together and glanced at Willow. She wanted to wipe away the smirk she wore with a kiss, but...

If anyone caught them, they would both be sanctioned.

Mags' heart ached as she pushed any thoughts of a kiss or possible sanction aside. She would take whatever punishment was dished out if it meant being with Willow, but she would never want to drag her friend through that.

The emperor three generations earlier had decreed that same-sex relationships were to be outlawed, as they would be *fruitless*. Nevermind the fact that fertility or adoption options were available for heterosexual couples who were unable to conceive due to infertility or sex organ variations. Apparently, the rule was good for some and not others. *Utter crap, of course,* Mags thought, but any dissenters were swiftly dealt with.

She was just about to hit Willow with an epic retort when the emperor lowered his arm as he peered around, surveying his minions with a chin tilt that spoke of the superiority complex he had been born with. "Greetings, men of the Worldship Honour. Thank you for assembling swiftly and calmly. It is with a sense of great regret that I gather you all today. But I come to you with dire news."

"Maintaining the remaining population of humanity was never the goal of the Worldship Honour. It was meant to be a temporary host whilst we fought back with the other nations to reclaim our planet." The emperor spoke clearly, slowly, but his tone grew deeper, which made something in Mags' gut twist. "As such, we have now reached a critical point. We are no longer able to manufacture the materials required to replace crucial parts in our oxygen and water systems. And, as you all know, without those two things, this ship cannot survive."

"Oh, crap..."

Mags internally echoed Willow's sentiment. That was terrible news. What were they supposed to do without those parts?

"The current estimates from engineering tell us that we have another two months, at best," the emperor dropped the new information as if it didn't hold the same destructive power as a nuclear missile.

Conversation tore through the room, the men all turning and speaking to those around them, yelling in shock and alarm, demanding more answers.

General Li, the leader of the Fenix armada, stepped forward and raised his hand for silence. "I know that this does not sound promising, but there is hope yet." Then, he gestured to the screens secured on the walls of the space, which flickered to life with a view of Earth. It rotated in space, a green and blue spheroid that looked far more innocuous than it was. Several generations ago, it had been filled with human life. Overfilled, some said. Regardless of the population debates, humanity thrived. Then, a hive of aliens warped into the system and overpowered the humans with a combination of surprise and air superiority.

The creatures were like those of nightmares; with armoured bodies and leathery wings, they reminded the people of the destructive, chaotic Hundun from ancient Chinese mythology. The years of the Great War were a brutal, deadly fight between the Hundun, or Huns as they were sometimes known, and the inhabitants of Earth.

Millions had died during the war, but even worse, the Huns began pumping noxious gas into Earth's atmosphere to make it more liveable for themselves. It created a thick blanket of toxicity on the surface of the planet, quickly making it inhospitable to humanity. Scientists had spent months trying to find the devices they presumed were generating the gas, but none were found, and it was assumed the creatures themselves were the source. Plans had been made to evacuate humankind before they all perished due to the poison.

Humanity had captured fallen Hun to study and understand how they worked together, the nations of Earth combining their efforts to create their own fighter ships to take on the Huns. Ships that could survive in the toxic atmosphere and interface with the human mind and react organically so they could finally catch up with the alien's air superiority. The ships were a mix of stolen alien biology and human technology. To honour the collaboration between the engineers from different nations who created the bird-like fighters, they were named Fenixes. The name paying homage to the Fenghuan, the mythological ruler of all birds, and the phoenix, the avian fire creature that is reborn from its own ashes.

The Fenixes proved to be extremely effective in combat

due to the addition of human weaponry; however, the Hun were too great in number and too spread out across the planet to effectively fight. When it was clear the Fenix fleet was not able to protect humanity, the nations panicked. Each continent had created its own Worldship to evacuate the civilians into space. However, launching through the Hundun-controlled atmosphere proved dangerous, and only the Worldship Honour survived.

The image of Earth on the screen zoomed in. It was a dizzying sight as the scope dove into the cloudy atmosphere and the ominous shadows of the aerial beasts shimmered through the toxic fog.

"The Hundun have started amassing in a single location. It is the first time their population has gathered in such a way, and it makes them prime targets for a full-scale ambush," General Li announced.

The cheers of reply were so loud that Mags had to turn down the volume on her device. The men pumped their fists into the air, and the cabinet ministers wore satisfied expressions at their enthusiasm. The emperor retrieved an electronic slate from one of his advisors as the cheers died down.

"As such," he said, continuing as if he hadn't paused, "All ship operations will be dependent on the needs of our pilots, and any ancillary operations will cease. All pilots, whether active or not, will be required to serve. Any retired pilots will be recalled upon the conscription conditions that at least one male of maturity must serve per household."

The emperor continued to rattle off conditions, but

they all sounded like gibberish to Mags. Her stomach was somewhere on the floor, and her heart hammered in her throat.

"Mags? Hey, Mags!" Willow's voice sounded a million miles away. *"Magnolia, speak to me!"*

Mags blinked and looked at the corner of the screen. Willow's face was so close to the camera all Mags could see was her eyes and nose. It would have been comical if she hadn't just realised that her father was the only man in her family who fit the requirements of the conscription notice... but he'd left the corps years earlier. At first, the doctors had suspected that he may have suffered neurological damage from a mission injury—the cause of his night terrors, low mood, irritability, and the way he trembled every time he heard reports of a new loss in the armada. However, when all the medical tests were exhausted, the psychological experts on board said it was most likely a condition of the mind. Other people in his old social circle had a hard time understanding the concept that her father had no visible injuries but was unable to fly, and she knew he carried a heavy load of shame and frustration over this.

Mags never understood the shame. For generations, they had given men no chance but to go to war and die, or watch their friends die. It was a brutal life, and she couldn't even imagine some of the horrors he had lived through. As much as he might try to hide it, she knew he was still struggling. The thought of him being forced back into a Fenix...

"Father!" The word slipped from her before she could stop it. Her hands flew to cover her mouth.

"Mags, it's going to be okay. He was deemed unfit to fly. They won't take him back!" The conviction in Willow's voice didn't register.

Despite Willow's attempt at reassuring her, Mags knew that he wasn't officially deemed unfit. According to regulations, only a physical injury excused a pilot from serving. However, her father's reputation, and his continued emotional difficulties, meant that he had been offered an honourable discharge to save his reputation. During a conscription, though? His excuse would no longer be valid.

It was different for Willow, Mags thought. Her older brother, Onyx, was one of the star pilots in his year. He was fit and healthy, and her father had retired with honour after an injury to his arm made it hard for him to pilot effectively. Nothing would change for her. There would be no added risk to their family.

But Mags?

"I can't lose him," she said, shaking her head. Her eyes burned as the emperor passed over to General Li to explain the training regimen they were setting up to account for the new and returned pilots.

"You won't," Willow promised. *"We'll come up with something, I swear."*

The next day, Willow and Mags were assigned duties.

They were supposed to be waiting for their marriage allocations. Traditionally, after women turned eighteen, they were granted six months off duties to *prepare for the commitment of marriage*. Then, when they were married, they oscillated between trying to conceive and birth two children and working to maintain the daily operation of the *Honour*. The men flew and then went home to help with conception. It was a dull, repetitive future that Mags wanted no part of.

Instead of going to the Matrimony and Household Preparation classes that they were supposed to attend, Willow, who had a penchant for all things tech, rigged their lesson systems with AI versions of themselves so people would still see their smiling faces on the screen even though they weren't there.

Which is exactly what they had done before the announcement was made about the Final Mission.

Mags stood in the cluttered living room of her tiny family apartment, batting her mother's hand away from the collar of her new green uniform for the millionth time. "I'm so proud of you. I always knew you would get into Medical," her mother crooned.

Pressing her lips together, Mags glanced at her father. He was unusually stoic as he sat in silence, his hand on his chin as he appeared lost in thought. He had barely said a word since returning home yesterday after the meeting, and Mags wondered if he had told her mother about the announcement.

Before she blurted out the question, she bit her lip. *Perhaps*, she thought to herself, *it's better if he doesn't.* If her father hadn't said anything yet, there was probably a good reason for it. Her mother worried a lot. It had been like that ever since the twins were born.

"I always thought she'd be in engineering," Mags' sister, Reed, said, putting down the shirt she was repairing for their grandmother.

Of course, her twin River couldn't help but chime in as well. "I thought her only hope was a good marriage match."

Mags rolled her eyes and ignored his jibe.

As annoying as the twins were, she did love them. Since their arrival pushed their family over the quota, the extra work their mother had to do had run her ragged. Their father was in a mundane, mindless job in the agriculture team that had him quiet and withdrawn whenever he was home. To make matters worse, their grandmother had to retire early due to ill health. Instead of having three working adults in the house, they had one, and instead of two kids, they had three.

"What do you think, Baba?" Mags asked, breaking him from his distraction.

"Oh." He looked as though he had to push hard to make his lips form a smile. "Very nice."

With a sigh, Mags stepped closer. "Can we speak, please?"

His thick, black eyebrows furrowed, but he nodded all the same.

Mags waited for her father to get up before she led the way to her room. Once they were both inside, she shut the door.

"Have you told Mama about the Final Mission?"

Worry flared in her father's eyes before he could blink it away. "Not yet. I will tell her when the time is right."

Mags pressed her lips together. "She would have heard the alarm. The ship will be riddled with whispers. Better she hear it from you."

Her father shook his head.

"You need to tell her, Baba," Mags insisted, lowering her voice and stepping in closer. Even with the door closed, she knew sound could travel between the two rooms if voices were loud enough or people were nosey enough. "You need to let her help you figure out how to get out of the conscription—"

"Get *out* of the conscription?" Her father's forehead creased, and his back stiffened. "Why would I do that?"

Mags' mouth flapped open and shut several times. What did he mean, *why*? As much as the family pretended they didn't hear his screams at night or ignored the way he woke with hollow, haunted eyes following a sleep riddled with night terrors, he was still having trouble living with what he saw. Going back would be dangerous.

"Because flying will get you killed!"

"Hush!" her father snapped at the ferocity in her tone. His cheeks flared with rage... or was that shame? "I must fly, Magnolia."

"I heard the whole announcement, Baba," Mags whisper-hissed, raising her hands. "I heard the terms of the conscription. I know that they require one man from each family, but surely this is different. There have to be exceptions for situations like—"

"Situations like what, Magnolia?"

She looked away, not wanting to finish the sentence anymore.

"It is my duty and honour to serve as a pilot. To protect our family and the future of humanity. I will not allow anyone to take that from me." Her father held his chin high and took a deep breath. "I will speak to Mama when the time is right. Until then, Magnolia, I expect you to respect my decision. You worry about your new job assignment. We will need as many trained medics as we can get when the battle begins."

Then, without giving her a chance to speak again, her father turned and walked out of the room. Magnolia saw River and Reed scrambling from where they must have been listening at the door. Everyone, including her grandmother, averted their eyes from her father's stony gaze but gawked at Mags as she walked out of the room.

She ignored the stares as she strode to the apartment door. "I'd better leave, I don't want to be late," she said, because lying was easier than acknowledging the conversation she'd just had with her father.

When the front door shut behind her, she slumped back against it and ran a hand through her hair.

She couldn't believe her father was going to obey the conscription notice. The pilots had to fly together as a squad. As skilled as her father might have been all those years ago, he was out of practice. Even if he could push through his constant fatigue, there was no telling how it would impact him to be back in the field. Besides, he had spent enough time risking his life and living with the consequences. As much as he felt he owed the colony something, if the ship was going down, her family would need him there with them, not sequestered off with the other pilots.

Mags meandered through the familiar, narrow maze of habitation corridors as she considered her options. The one thing she knew for certain was that she would not allow her father to answer that conscription notice. The thought of him putting himself into that situation again broke her heart, and she worried it might just break her mother's heart, too.

By the time she stopped outside a familiar door, Mags had made a decision. With a new sense of resolve, she raised her hand to knock, but the door slid open, and she was met by Willow's smiling face. She shoved her hands into the pockets of her scrubs to avoid the urge to hug her friend in greeting. They couldn't afford to do that in the corridors.

Instead, she said, "Grey suits you," as she looked Willow up and down.

"Grey doesn't suit anyone." Willow raised an eyebrow at her as she self-consciously adjusted the grey engineering overalls on her short but curvy frame. "Do we have time to hang out before you have to report to medical?"

"We do, and we need to talk. Is anyone home?"

"Nope, I've got the place to myself, as usual."

"Great."

Mags slipped past Willow to enter her family's apartment. It was much neater than Mags'. Even though it was the same size, it only had to house Willow and her folks. Her brother had moved out a few years ago when he got married, and her grandparents still had their own apartment, as they were both working. As a result, it was neat in a way Mags envied, and it was usually also quiet.

"Hey, what's going on?" Willow gently rested her hand on Mags' arm.

She paused, taking a breath. "My father is planning to obey the conscription notice."

"Ah…" Willow bit her lip. "I've been doing a bit of snooping. I managed to get into the administration network and saw a whole bunch of protest letters that were denied. People with bionic limbs, damaged sight, single fathers with two children to look after… no one is being granted exemption."

The news blew some of the steam out of Mags, but she

had been prepared for that in some ways. She had seen the look on the emperor's face. He was determined. "I know the admin servers are one of your favourites to snoop around in. Any chance you can get into people's personal files?"

"Oh, that's easy." Willow shrugged as she sank onto the couch and watched Mags. "Why?"

"Any chance you can get in there and change my assigned sex?"

Willow blinked. "You want me to do *what*?"

Mags sat down beside her and leaned forward. "Change my sex to male and cancel my job assignment. I'll take my father's place for the conscription."

Silence fell between them as a range of emotions played over Willow's face. "That's ludicrous."

"No, it isn't." Mags pointed to the simulator in the corner of the living room. "We've been hacking into those and running sim flights for over a decade. I'm good at flying."

"You're a wildcard at flying, is what I know. Plus, there's no way anyone is going to look at you and think *you're* a man." Willow surveyed Mags. "You're far too pretty."

"Then I'll make a pretty man." Mags leaned in. "Please, Willow. I need to do this, and it will be so much more diffi-cult without your help."

"*Without* my help?"

"I'm doing it either way."

The two stared at each other. It was a standoff. Willow was clearly trying to test Mags' resolve, but there was no way she was going to budge. She was serious. If something happened to her, her family wouldn't miss her. She was probably going to be forced to marry and move out soon anyway. If they survived this fight, that is.

With a groan, Willow sagged against the worn cushions of her couch and ran a hand through her hair. "Say I do manage to change your file, what then?"

"I can take my father's old flight suit," Mags said, the plan forming in her mind as she spoke. "I'll have to go to the market to get new parts so it will interface with the flight units. I'll have to cut my hair as well."

"And what about your family, what will you tell them?"

Mags' eyes widened. "I can't tell them. They'd do whatever they could to stop me."

"So, what... you just sneak out of the house in the middle of the night and don't tell anyone where you're going?" Willow shook her head at the idea.

Mags was far too close to her family for that.

Which was why it was *perfect*.

"I'll leave a note."

Willow just stared at her, dumbstruck. Mags didn't blame her. It was a wild plan. Instead of arguing, her friend grabbed her electronic slate and got to work, muttering all sorts of things about *stupid ideas* and *death wishes*.

THREE

Mags checked over the list on her digital slate one last time. She and Willow had worked together to plan what she would need in addition to the basic requirements demanded in the conscription notice. Trips to each of the markets on the ship had gotten Mags what she needed: an updated network chip for her father's old flight suit from the starboard market, sleeping bag and training clothes from the port-side supply store, copper connection wires from the engineering vaults in the stern, and a sharp pocketknife for self-protection from the bow.

After confirming she had everything, Mags had shoved it all into her pack, adding a few essential supplies and plain, baggy clothing. She only had one thing left to add: her father's flight suit. It had been a while since he had pulled it out to show her and her siblings, but she remembered him tucking it away in the wardrobe of the room he shared with her mother and grandmother. She hoped he hadn't moved it.

Reed and River were restless sleepers but rarely woke from their tossing and turning for anything short of an emergency klaxon. That made it easy enough for Mags to slip out of bed, fully dressed, and tiptoe toward the door. The living room was dark as she made her way through, thankful that her family were heavy sleepers. Still, it was close to four in the morning as she approached the door to her parent's room and pressed the panel for it to open. She bit her lip at the electronic hiss and waited to make sure there were no more noises inside before creeping in.

Both bedrooms in the apartment had identical layouts, so Mags was able to blindly make her way to the wardrobe. Her mother's gentle snores sounded through the room, interspersed by an occasional whimper or nightmarish protest from her father. The first time he made one of the noises, she froze. However, when she identified it for what it was, she let out a breath of relief and continued.

Unfortunately, the inside of the wardrobe was a mess. Groping around, she felt all sorts of textures and shapes, and all she could think was that she had to hurry up and get the uniform. She still had so much to do before the conscription draft at eight o'clock.

"Finally!" she groaned with relief as her fingers slid over the slippery fabric of the flight suit. In her mind, she pictured the black and bronze overalls as she gently dislodged them from the Gordian knot of clothing. Then she carefully shut the wardrobe and turned back toward the door.

"Going somewhere?"

A pair of eyes flashed in the darkness, and Mags' heart imploded in her chest.

She brought a hand up to cover her mouth to muffle her sudden panting and shook her head as she looked at her grandmother, still laying in her bunk. Shrouded in shadows as she was, it was hard to see the lines of her wizened face and impossible to determine what her expression was.

"No—"

"No need to lie," her grandmother interrupted, sounding more lucid than usual but also tired. "You and your parents think I see nothing. I do…"

Mags bit the inside of her lip to keep herself from talking. Her father no longer talked in his sleep, and she had a feeling that if her mother stopped snoring, that would be the end of her adventure.

"Oh, don't worry. I'm not going to stop you. We all used to sneak out at your age," her grandmother tutted. "Just stay safe, girl."

Relief flooded through Mags, and she edged toward the door. "I love you, Maa Maa," she whispered. "Please take care of them."

The words slipped out before she could stop them, but her grandmother didn't argue. Instead, Mags made it to the living room, where she shoved the flight suit into her pack. Then, instead of hanging around to see if her grandmother would change her mind, Mags fled the apartment.

The ship corridors still had a fair amount of light as she made her way to Willow's apartment. It was just in case people were returning from night shifts or there was an emergency. It was a bit of an assault on Mags' eyes after the near perfect darkness of her family's rooms, but she adjusted just as she turned into the corridor where Willow's apartment was.

"What are you doing out here?" Mags hissed, seeing her best friend sitting outside her front door.

Willow yawned as she got to her feet. "Didn't want you ringing the doorbell and wake my folks." She reached back and opened the door. "Come on, let's hurry. We have a lot to do."

FOUR

An hour and a half later, Mags zipped up her father's old flight suit. It fit surprisingly well, given the fact it hadn't been made her for. She looked down at herself and shifted, feeling the smallest bit of resistance along the inside of her sleeves and pants where Willow had sewn in the new neural conduits.

"How do I look?"

"Good, but…" Willow bit her lip as she dragged her critical gaze over Mags, drumming her fingers on the desk she was sitting beside. "We need to do something about your hair."

Mags sighed. She had been waiting for this. Whilst women were required to have their hair a certain length past their shoulders, men had to have theirs cut short. Nothing was allowed to hang below the length of their ear. It was far shorter than Mags had ever imagined going, even in her wildest daydreams, but it was necessary.

"Lucky you've got scissors then." Mags gestured to the short-bladed shears that sat on Willow's desk.

Willow rested her hands over the scissors and scrunched up her nose as she met Mags' gaze. "So... we're really doing this, then?"

"Uh, yes." Mags frowned. "That's why we've been doing all of this work."

Getting to her feet, the scissors in hand, Willow sighed. "Yeah, but now it's more real." She shook her head. "Hurry up and get your butt in that seat before I change my mind about this."

A smile tugged at Mags' lips as she did as she was told. She sat straight and made sure all her hair was pulled out of the collar of her suit as Willow got to work.

The first snip was the most nerve-wracking. After that, there was no going back. Emerging now with short hair would get Mags in a great deal of trouble, so she had little choice but to continue. Willow was quiet as she cut Mags' hair, apparently concentrating hard.

"You're lucky I've been cutting my father's hair for years," she said, shaking her head.

After another ten minutes, she was done.

Mags got to her feet and walked over to the mirror in the room. When she stepped in front of it, she did a double take.

Staring back at her was a pilot.

She reached up, running her hand over her short hair and marvelling at how bristly it was. "Oh, wow..."

Willow stepped up behind her, and Mags met her gaze in the reflection.

"Okay, I have to say, you actually make a pretty hot guy," Willow said, a sparkle of amusement in her eyes.

Mags cocked an eyebrow at her. "Oh? I was kinda hoping that I was hot as a girl too, but…" she trailed off, watching the way Willow's cheeks turned a pretty shade of pink.

"You make a hot girl, too," Willow conceded, resting her hand on Mags' shoulder.

Her fingers were warm, even through the fabric of the flight suit, and Mags wanted to stand like that forever.

"Please be careful out there, Mags," Willow said, leaning so close that her breath was tickling Mags' neck. "I know we'll only have like a month left if this doesn't succeed, but I can't imagine living through it knowing that something had already happened to you. You have to survive. I… I need you."

Mags' breath caught in her throat at those tender words. At the way she could feel the heat of Willow's body along her back. At the new intensity in her eyes. She turned her face to say something, but her lips brushed against Willow's.

A gasp slipped from Willow's lips, and her hand tensed on Mag's shoulder. Then, she seemed to sag against her back, and she leaned in closer.

Spinning and wrapping her arms around her best friend, Mags deepened the kiss with a soft gasp. She'd never kissed anyone before. If she'd known it felt this good, maybe she would have done it sooner.

She wasn't sure whether the kiss lasted a breath or an eternity, but either way, it ended far too soon. When

Willow pulled away from her, breathless and flushed, she rested her forehead on Mags'. "That was…"

"Amazing," Mags completed, stealing another gentle kiss.

"Stay. Please."

The quiet plea made Mags' heart cleave in two. But as much as she wanted to give in, the kiss and the way Willow gently traced her soft fingertips over Mags' cheek only strengthened her resolve to leave. Not only did she need to protect her family, but she also had to protect her best friend.

"I wish I could," she said. It wasn't a lie. "But I have skills my father has lost. I'm not arrogant enough to believe I'm any better than the other serving pilots, but a single person may make a difference."

"I should come."

The idea made Mags wince. Willow was every bit as good on the simulator as Mags was, but the thought of her getting into a flight suit and connecting her life to that of a bio-mechanical beast for real felt too risky.

"I need you here." Mags shook her head. "I may need someone with the skills to surf the networks to save my arse at some point, and you're the only person I would trust."

A soft *beep-beep, beep-beep* sounded through the room, and it made both Mags and Willow tense.

"Where did all the time go?" Willow's quiet voice was laced with panic.

"I wish I knew," Mags agreed, but she reached up to gently brush her thumb over Willow's lips. "I also wish I knew about this sooner, too. Is this something you want to continue?"

"Are you kidding?" Willow sighed, a breath of pure longing. "I never want it to end."

Mags kissed her again. It was nowhere near as deep or as long as she wanted it to be, but the passion was undeniable. "Then I'm sorry we didn't figure it out sooner. It's always been you, Willow. Always will be."

Before Mags could question her choice, she stepped back. The places where her own body had been in contact with Willow's suddenly felt cold and distant. She took a slow, steadying breath. "I'll see you soon."

"That's the only outcome I will accept," Willow said, biting her lip and wrapping her arms around herself the way she did when she was sad or lonely. "Go, before I change my mind. I'll get on the network and fix up your profile so you'll fit the conscription notice criteria. It will be sorted before you get there."

There were so many things Mags wanted to say, but the words got stuck in her throat. Instead, she just nodded, stepped back, picked up her bag from the floor by her feet, then turned and left Willow's room, hoping it wouldn't be the last time she saw her best friend.

CHAPTER

FIVE

Despite feeling as though her time with Willow was shortened, Mags followed the thick, thrumming pipeline known as the Yellow River, named after a river that ran through China, the country from where the *Honour* took off. Like the Earth version, this pipeline was the source of nourishment for everything around it. It carried critical flow of air, water, and power from the front to the back of the ship, with hundreds of branches winding off from the main course to feed the rest of the *Honour*.

As Mags approached the aft of the ship, she pictured her father rising from his bed and walking to his wardrobe to retrieve his flight suit. She could only imagine the chaos that would ensue when it was found missing. Her mother would wake to help him look, whilst her grandmother sat and watched, most likely amused. The noise would draw the attention of Reed and River, and then someone would notice her own absence.

Mags hoped her parents would find the message she left them before she departed. She had a feeling it wouldn't be enough for them, but to risk chasing her down would seal her punishment and potentially bring dishonour on her whole family for the deception. She pictured the look of realisation and resignation on her father's face. Mags knew he would be disappointed in her but also in himself, but... at least he would stay alive for as long as possible.

When Mags reached the elevator that travelled between levels, she knew going down would lead her to the engines, and up to the hangar. She sighed and pressed the *up* arrow just as footsteps sounded on the deck behind her. Turning around, a group of three young men her age were jogging toward her.

Or, rather, toward the elevator.

"Hold it for us!" one of the young men called out, voice gruff and commanding.

Mags immediately disliked his tone, and the way his eyes narrowed at her when she didn't immediately reply. It wasn't that she didn't want to. She would have happily tested how fast he could run, but she was frozen in place and suddenly far too conscious of the fact her hair was short and her breasts were bound tightly beneath her flight suit. What if they saw right through her pathetic disguise?

The door pinged open behind her, and she stepped back to board the elevator. There were already several men inside, all in similar black and bronze suits and holding bags, their ages ranging from late twenties to early sixties, if Mags guessed correctly, none of them looked pleased about having to hold the door for three young men who clearly were unable to arrive on time.

Mags reached forward, fingers hovering over the operational buttons for the door.

"Hold it!" the young man demanded again.

Jabbing her finger against the *Hold* button, Mags stepped aside. One of the older men grumbled, but the three younger ones tumbled onto the elevator, the final one panting a thanks as he hitched his bag up higher on his shoulder.

"One hopes your flying is better than your time management," a mid-forties man said, eyes narrowed.

The latecomers all stood a little straighter at the rebuke. The one who had demanded they hold the elevator met the gaze of the speaker as he jabbed his finger against the hangar button. "It is," he said, chin held high. "It keeps everyone on their toes. Even the bogies. Can't keep giving them the same *old* tired tactics."

Several tuts sounded in the elevator, but the younger group ignored them.

Mags sighed and let her arm drop to her side, relieved, as no one seemed to question who she was or say anything about how she looked. She supposed she had the latecomers to thank for taking any attention off her for the ride to the hangar. As her concern temporarily waned, the feeling of Willow's lips on hers floated back to her mind, and Mags wished she could turn back time. Wished she could return to her best friend's apartment.

Any wishes were wiped away as the elevator doors opened to a cacophony of noise and flurry of activity.

Mags gawked about with wonder. The ship had two hangars: one for the Fenix ships and one for the pods. She had never been allowed in the pod hangar. It was heavily guarded because if people were to access it, they could access the ships. As a child, however, she had been on an excursion to see the ships in the Fenix hangar. Mags found it just as impressive now as she had back then. The Fenixes stood like silent sentinels, plucked straight from myths of old.

Sitting upright with their feathery wings curled against their sides, the Fenixes reached almost sixty feet tall. Unlike their mythical counterparts, though, they had thick armour plating surrounding the upper parts of their face, neck, and torso. Lighter protections intermittently covered their wings. All of this was designed to give them an edge, even in melee combat when facing the Hun up close. Affixed to the torso were the missile pods, flush against the body. Whenever a missile was launched, small doors would open, allowing the projectiles to fly outward when required. The rail guns were attached to the back of the Fenix, melded with the back plate armour at the firing ports and the front point of the wing. The head was entirely artificial, designed to be bird-like in the same fashion as the birds of legend, and all the advanced avionics and neural link systems were situated in this location. Whenever the Fenix was operational, its eyes glowed a bright red.

The men all streamed through the gaps between ships, almost oblivious to the incredible pieces of technology around them.

"Name?" an officer demanded of the three boys who were in the car with her as they stepped out of the elevator.

Mags joined the line just in time to hear the officer confirm the given names of the young men as Cliff, Shale, and Ash. They were all sent to a section of the hangar that seemed to hold younger people with new-looking pilot jumpsuits. None of the older men that had travelled with her were wearing theirs yet, but they all carried well-stuffed duffel bags.

"You came prepared," the officer noted, nodding at Mags' uniform.

"Uh, pardon?" Mags blurted. Then she realised her voice was entirely too high. She thumped her fist against her bound chest and coughed. "Sorry, dry throat. Pardon?"

The man frowned at her but gestured to her suit again. "That looks like it's older than you. Good luck gift from your father? Don't worry, you're not the only one," the officer said, sounding bored. "Name?"

"Hua Marsh," Mags said, the name tasting off on her tongue.

Time slowed to a near backward crawl as the captain scrolled down his list. Then he looked up and smiled faintly. "My father served with the great Hua Zhou." Mags gulped at hearing her father's name. "He died in the Canyon Crisis. He would have been proud to know how many people he saved under your father's guidance. I heard your father retired following that mission. I trust he is well?"

Mags' mind flicked back to her father before she left, fitfully fighting against unrelenting enemies in his constant night terrors. She forced a solemn smile and a nod. It had been so long since she had thought of her father as anyone other than the man he had been over the past few years. The admiration in the officer's eyes was an odd turn of events.

"Good. You'll be with the other lads your age. You're all just receiving your first assignments today." He gestured to the group where the trio of young men were now talking and laughing, pushing each other about, oblivious to the inconvenience they were causing the people around them.

"Thank you, officer," Mags hitched her bag up on her shoulder and walked over, tucking her chin and skirting around the edge of the group of young men, not wanting to draw attention.

It was lucky for her that General Li appeared at that moment, stepping up onto a stage made of stacked crates toward the far end of the hangar. When he spoke, his voice echoed, magnified by speakers built into the walls of the vast space. "Greetings, men of Worldship Honour. Thank you for your promptness in response to the Conscription Notice. It is with great pride in our ship that I can look over you and know you have all responded with a sense of duty and discipline."

A snort sounded just to Mags' left, where Cliff and his cronies were standing. Even though she wasn't the greatest fan of discipline, she was surprised at how arrogant Cliff seemed and wished she had paid more attention the social hierarchies and politics on board. She could just imagine he was some smug diplomat's son.

"The officers by the elevator have sorted you into your

squadrons. Our current pilots will remain in their usual squads. Please treat the men around you like your new family. You will train with them, eat with them, sleep with them, and fight with them. There is also a very real chance you will die with them. Therefore, I ask that you conduct yourselves with the distinct honour that comes with your position. Despite the dire odds, I have faith this final push has a chance to free our people and return us to the planet that was stolen from us."

A cheer rattled through the hangar. Mags joined in, albeit belatedly. She pumped her fist in the air and focused on keeping her voice as deep as possible. When the cheer was over, the same captain who had assigned her to the group by the elevator called for attention. He rattled off a list of names and unit groupings, and the movement of people around her felt choreographed as men dodged and danced around each other on their way to stand under signs that were hung high on the hangar walls. Each was a simple, symbolic depiction of some element or object, such as a forest, fire, river, typhoon, or a moon.

When *Hua Marsh* was called out, Mags didn't respond right away. She peered around, feeling stupid for not knowing there was someone on the ship with the same family name as her. Then she jolted into action as she remembered that it was *her* name.

Mags' gaffe went unnoticed thanks to everyone being distracted as they tried to organise themselves. With the number of captains trying to get the men to where they needed to be, it was hard to hear or see what was going on. As she headed toward the wall, she figured they were just hoping for the best and would catch any stragglers later. She silently made her way over to where she was told to go as more and more names were called. It was at least a few minutes before someone joined her under the moon poster.

"Ah, we meet again. I hope you're more assertive in the cockpit than you were in that elevator." Cliff clapped Mags on the shoulder. He was the shortest and stockiest of the boys, but clearly the most confident.

Mags choked on a cough at the force of the pat and had to quickly cover it with a deep chortle. "Hopefully you're on time for the battle," Mags retorted, knowing that bantering was one of the prime ways young men her age interacted.

To her satisfaction, Cliff pressed his lips together and narrowed his eyes at her jape. He clearly hadn't been expecting her to reply, and she was pleased to have thrown him off guard. At least until she saw Shale and Ash saunter over to join them. Ash was the tallest of the three, and looked as though he could be toppled over by a slight breeze. Shale was just a bit shorter, but he had a handsome face that Mags knew the girls would fight over.

The other two young men distracted Cliff from Mags as they all patted each other on the backs and made foolish jokes. Before any of them could turn on her, they were joined by a young man in a captain's uniform. Mags bit the inside of her cheek as she recognised him.

Talon.

The son of General Li.

Mags shrank back behind Cliff as Willow's brother's

best friend approached. The two had been in the same training cohort and had gone on to win many important skirmishes with their skill. Mags had run into him several times at Willow's family apartment, but he had hardly spared her a glance. She only hoped her disguise was good enough that he didn't give her a second look this time either.

The arrival of such a well-known pilot had the three foolish young men near her fall silent, especially as their attention snagged on the sling his arm was in. Talon adjusted his posture, and from the way his square jaw was set, everyone around him knew that mentioning his arm would be a bad idea.

"Good morning, Moon Squadron." Talon's voice was just as smooth and confident as Mags had remembered. "I have been assigned as the officer in charge of overseeing your training, getting you ready to join the more experienced pilots in battle. We have one month before we are expected to join the others in the sky. By the looks of it, we have a lot of work to do. Follow me, we don't have time to waste."

The tone Talon used indicated that he was not keen on the job. Mags couldn't really blame him. Judging by the way he kept his sling-supported arm tightly against his firm chest, he had been given it because he was unable to fly. In any other scenario, he would be given leave to recuperate at home with his wife, but the conscription call must have meant that he couldn't be spared from the war effort.

Most of the other groups were still milling about

having discussions with their own captains, and no one seemed to pay them any mind as they followed Talon through the maze of bodies and Fenixes. He led them out of Hangar One and into a network of hallways beyond until they reached a room labelled "Training Hall". Inside, there was a central, open space, and the walls were lined with simulator pods. Instead of taking them straight to the simulators, Talon walked them to the middle of the hall. The floor of the internal section was a lighter grey in colour than the standard metal plating, and when Mags stepped onto it, there was a slight, spongy bounce on the surface beneath her feet, much like the gym. Also similar to the gym, the room smelled like it usually held too many sweaty bodies in too small a space.

"For the next four weeks, this will be your home." Talon stopped and rounded on them, and Mags jumped back to avoid running into him. "You will eat when I tell you, sleep when I tell you, and crap when I tell you."

"He's joking, right?" Shale whispered to the others behind Mags' back.

"I am not joking." Talon skirted around Mags and stood before Shale. "And the next time you have something to say, you will speak aloud to the group. Am I clear?"

"Yes, sir," Shale responded meekly.

"I didn't hear you." Talon towered over Shale, his features hardening.

Shale straightened but couldn't hide the tremble in his stance. "Yes, sir!"

Talon nodded approvingly. Then he gestured for them to form a line and started to pace back and forth in front of them. When his back was to her, Mags took the opportunity to get a good look at the state-of-the-art flight suit he was wearing. "Now, I understand that you have all completed basic training. So, you probably think you're the best. But you're not. Basic is for little boys who still play with toys. Only real men survive actual battles."

Mags snorted. She was neither boy nor man, but she had every intention of succeeding in battle.

Freezing on the spot at the end of the line, Talon whipped around "What was that?"

The group remained silent, but Mags swore she felt Ash trembling beside her. She half-expected one of the others to tattle on her, but they kept their mouths shut.

Talon shook his head and sighed. "You're the saddest bunch I've ever met." His hand whipped out, snatching up Mags by the collar and dragging her closer.

When she met his razor gaze, she knew beyond a doubt that he was aware she was the one who had laughed.

Talon leaned in closer, his breath hot on her face as he hissed, "I'll make a man out of you yet." With a look of utter distain, he pushed her away. She stumbled over her own feet and fell flat on her arse. "Now, all of you. Drop and give me thirty."

"Thirty?" Cliff stuttered, confused.

"Burpees, you idiot." He pointed to the ground.

Mags, for one, was already down, so it was easy for her to transition into position. At least her stupid laugh had gotten her that much.

Talon started counting them through the exercise, and Mags had to stop herself from groaning. Sure, she had done physical sessions with the other young women, but there was never a focus on strength like there had been for the boys. Her body was burning within no time, sweat beading on her brow.

The others seemed just as unimpressed to be doing the burpees as Mags was, even if they didn't seem quite as breathless as her. When Talon's back was facing them, Cliff whispered to the others, "I bet pretty boy hasn't done a burpee properly in his life."

"I'm sorry, did someone say something?" Talon paused his counting and glared at them.

Cliff shoved Mags in front of them, offering her as tribute. Mags coughed a little to clear her voice and straightened her shoulders. "Uh, we were just wondering why the burpees? We use our minds to control the Fenixes."

Talon narrowed his eyes as though trying to determine whether her question was genuine or not. In the end, he glanced at Ash and then crossed his arms over his chest. "Something you didn't learn in basic is that the neural interface connecting you to your Fenix mimics the same neural pathways used to move your own body. So, the better you understand your own body and its limitations, the better you will understand your bird. That's why from now on, every morning before any other training, you will complete one hundred burpees and a ten-kilometre run on the treadmills. As a matter of fact, you should start that run right now."

Mags found the run to be less of an issue than the burpees. In this area, she was able to cope better than the men beside her. They dialled their speed up too high at the start, most likely to try and impress Talon, but Mags kept her pace steady and managed to finish before all of them.

When they were finally done, Talon walked over. "Oh, good. The cardio didn't kill you. I'm glad, I would have hated to fill out the paperwork." Without waiting for them to catch their breath, he moved on to the next room.

"Your performance so far is mediocre at best. However, we don't have time to linger, so we will be moving on to combat training," Talon announced as the four recruits stood by the sims, catching their breath after their morning run.

Cliff cheered. "Yes! Finally, we get to shoot something!"

The others laughed, but the look on Talon's face had them all swallowing their mirth with audible gulps.

"Oh... you're going to shoot us." Cliff hung his head.

"No." It was Talon's turn to chuckle. "Tell me, Private Cliff. What is the AIM-500?"

"Uh..."

Mags wanted to jump in, but Shale beat her to it. "It's the primary long-range missile equipped to the Fenix. Radar guided, it has a range of one hundred nautical miles, max speed Mach six."

"Well done, Shale. How many do you carry?"

"Four, sir."

"How about the AIM-320?"

"Medium range, heat seeking," Ash started, before Talon cut in.

"How many?"

"Three, sir."

"How many rounds does the XRM-20 rail gun carry?" Talon turned his piercing gaze on Mags.

She shifted uncomfortably, still not liking when people watched her too closely. "600 bolts... sir." She was confused as to his point.

"Correct, Marsh. I can see you have all been studying." Then, he crossed his uninjured arm over his sling. "What happens when all of your munitions are depleted?"

"Return to base?" Cliff replied hesitantly.

"You would abandon the mission? Run like a scared little girl?"

"No, sir!" he replied quickly.

Approval flashed in Talon's eyes. "Our Fenixes are equipped with some of the most advanced weaponry known to civilisation. They can eliminate targets without you even needing to see them, but the Huns have numbers on their side. When you run out of those fancy pea shooters, the only thing you have left are these." Talon raised his uninjured arm and flexed it.

Shale balked at the suggestion. "You want us to punch them?"

"Yes, Private. I want you to punch them. I want you to punch them so hard, they will be the ones crying to their mothers."

"The aliens don't have matriarchal figures, sir. They operate as a hive mind, although some have speculated that there might be..." Ash chimed in.

Mags pressed her lips together to hide her amusement as Talon cut him off with a single raised eyebrow in question.

Ash cleared his throat. "Uh, I mean... we'll punch them, sir."

"That's what I thought. Now, for the rest of today, Moon Squadron, we will be sparring." Talon directed their attention to the spring floor in the middle of the room. A robotic training dummy stood in the centre, and Talon activated the automaton with a switch. It came to life, arms up and ready for battle.

For the next few hours, he taught them basic defensive and offensive manoeuvres on the sparing mat, focusing on close quarter grappling techniques, stating that the Huns and the Fenix would end up in a fight like that in the air. They spent an entire day training, being thrown around by a machine. They learned several different techniques—the clawhold, ironhold, shoulder claw, and, Mags' least favourite, the mandible claw. It caused genuine pain, and at one point she thought her jaw was being ripped from her head. Talon impressed upon them the importance of technique. The Hun fought with the ferocity of untrained animals, but they lacked coordination and focus. If the boys could master the style and form, then strength and numbers would no longer be an advantage.

Mags had bruises forming all over her body and was aching in places she didn't even know existed.

CHAPTER

SIX

Following the full day of training, Talon showed Moon Squadron to their quarters. Well, Mags thought quarters was an optimistic word for the old storage room that had been converted into a sleeping room. There were four uncomfortable looking temporary cots set up in the space, almost on top of each other. Each had a pillow, a threadbare blanket, and a rough looking towel on the end. Their assigned bathroom was farther down the corridor, but it looked as though they would be sharing it with at least three other squadrons.

"Every night, you will have dinner in the mess hall with the rest of the men, and then you will return here," Talon explained, hanging back at the door and looking around the grungy excuse for a room with undisguised disdain. "Following that, you will be expected to get to bed at a respectable hour and be up bright and early for training in the morning. Some of the older pilots may find other ways to… entertain themselves during their evenings, but please know that I will have none of that from you."

"So… we eat, then sleep, then wash, and repeat?" Shale asked, features falling as he blinked back at Talon. "Can't we go visit our families? Spend some time playing games or catching up on news?"

Talon shook his head. "That is a privilege afforded to the men who know how to fight. And fly. And work together as a team. You lot need all the training you can get. You are not to go out and become distracted, and I don't want you sauntering onto the combat mat in the mornings nursing a hangover and zoning out because you've had two hours of sleep."

Cliff, Ash, and Shale seemed mortified by Talon's order. As much as Mags hated it, she was somewhat relieved. She had already told herself that it would be too dangerous to contact her family, lest her ruse be discovered, so Talon's orders provided an easy excuse for not attempting to leave the barracks.

As the other three stood, mouths flopping open uselessly, Mags gave Talon a salute. "Understood, sir," she said. Then she walked to the bed closest to the door and snatched up the towel. Outside in the corridor, she could already hear the intermittent buzz of passing conversation as the pilots made their way to the cafeteria for dinner. Given that she would be sharing the hygiene facilities with so many men, she hoped she could get in early while they were all busy with something else.

Just before Mags could turn to leave, Talon frowned at

her, his eyebrows almost knitting together. "Marsh, what do you think you are doing?"

Mags blinked. "Uh, hitting the showers, sir," she said, trying to keep her tone respectful even though she thought it was obvious. What else would she be doing with the towel?

"Not now you aren't. It's dinner time. It is expected that all pilots attend the meal, as it is the time where messages from the General and the Emperor will be disseminated," Talon informed her.

"Oh." The hope of no longer smelling like a pile of dirty gym towels drained out of Mags. Especially as she realised she would be walking right into, and eating with, a group of men who probably also smelled like piles of dirty gym towels. The thought made her gag a bit.

"You feeling okay, Marsh?" Cliff asked, although there was more amusement in his voice than genuine concern.

"Of course." Mags straightened up and threw the towel back on the bed. "Why wouldn't I be?" She held her chin high as she caught his gaze, challenging him to say more.

Talon pinched the bridge of his nose with his good hand and shook his head. "Just get out there. And don't carry on like petulant toddlers in the mess. It's bad enough that I've been made to babysit you lot, don't make me look like a fool in front of the others."

Before any of them could argue, Talon turned and led the way out of the room, leaving them to scramble after him.

It was a short walk to the cafeteria, but when the small group arrived, most of the tables were already full. Magnolia, like most people aboard the *Honour*, ate her meals in her apartment with her family. Seeing so many men gathered in the cafeteria made her feel awfully crowded. At least in the hangar earlier they had been spread amongst the Fenixes, but here?

Well, she had been right to be concerned about the gym towel smell. Even the aroma of the dinner that was being served did nothing to neutralise the stench.

"Late again, I see?" came a disgruntled voice from a table by the door. Magnolia looked over to find the same man who had been in the elevator eyeing the group with disdain.

"Pardon our intrusion." Talon bowed to him respectfully. "This way, men." He glared at Mags and the others and guided them away from the tables near the door, where pilots were already trying to enjoy their evening meal.

They made their way around the outskirts of the cafeteria to find that the only table left was right beside the bins, the floor nearby sticky with drying splatters of soup that hadn't quite made it into the food recycler on the wall.

Before anyone could comment on the location they had little choice but to take, a door to the far side of the cafeteria, right beside the servery, opened.

"General Li!" Ash spluttered.

Talon winced as he looked over, then reached out, grabbing Ash's arm, and dragged him into a seat. "Get down, all of you!" he warned.

The young men scrambled to comply. Mags include.

Before General Li's entry, the cafeteria had been abuzz

with light conversation. All of that settled into a tense silence as the leader of the military, and Talon's father, cleared his throat and called for attention.

"Good evening, men. It is just as much an honour to see you all here tonight as it was this morning. I have heard excellent reports from all of our captains, and am aware that it has been a productive day of training and orientation." Li let that sit for a moment as he waved his arm out in a wide gesture to those gathered. "I have spent my time with our intelligence department, tracking the movements of the Hundun horde. Their migration patterns are commensurate with our predictions, and it means that our call to form a final attack was a sound decision."

Li's words had the men enthralled, and as much as Mags wanted to be just as excited as the others, she couldn't help but think the experienced soldier was laying it all on a little too thick. They all knew why they were here, and he wasn't giving them anything new. Anything other than "We are right, keep following our command."

As she sat and listened to the speech, she had to resist the urge to yawn. It had been such an intense forty-eight hours for her, and she was exhausted. Really, all she wanted to do was clean up and curl into her cot.

Just as Mags was about to write off the General's entire monologue as propaganda and forced motivation, he gestured with a wide sweep of his arm toward a series of screens that lined the far wall of the cafeteria. They flared to life to reveal a complex looking table with the name of all the squadrons in the first column and statistics like the captain's name, the number of pilots, and whether they were battle ready in the others.

The first ten squadrons were already listed as approved for battle.

Mags joined the others in Moon Squadron as they leaned forward, peering at the board.

"Where are we?" Shale asked, face falling as General Li scrolled farther and farther down the list.

"A place I trust we will not be for long," Talon muttered, keeping his shoulders straight and chin high despite the way men at other tables turned to look at him questioningly when his father finally stopped scrolling to reveal that Moon Squadron was right down at the bottom of the list.

"As the days progress," General Li said, calling attention back to himself, "we expect more and more squadrons to be added as airworthy to our armada. Until your team has been listed as airworthy, we expect you to do nothing but eat, sleep, and train. There will be no recreation hours or visits to your families until we know you are in fighting shape. We do not have long before the attack. So, train well, and make your ancestors proud."

Mags swore under her breath as General Li's face turned until he was looking directly at Talon. She gulped, resisting the urge to turn toward her captain. She was still recovering from her shock at the way his father had eyed him in front of everyone when the older man turned and left the room. Pilots from other tables all gawked at the son of the General, and Talon ignored them all.

"You'd all better go and get your food. You will need the energy tomorrow," he said to his squadron.

The tension at the table was palpable enough that they all got to their feet without arguing. Mags ignored the amused titters that followed her and the others to the servery. They got a tray each and loaded it with watered down soup and dumplings. It wasn't the best food, but Mags wasn't going to complain.

When the group returned to their table, Talon was deep in conversation with another man who had taken Mags' seat.

Talon's smile grew strained as he noticed their approach. He gestured to his companion and said, "Men, this is—"

"Onyx!" Ash gasped, awe in his tone.

Mags froze on the spot as the man turned around.

As *Willow's brother* turned around.

Onyx's dark, familiar eyes raked over the other young men and, in a state of panic, Mags let out a grunt and dropped her tray. Ash, Cliff, and Shale all cursed and jumped to the side as her bowl dropped to the floor and sprayed the area with scalding soup and projectile dumplings.

"Aiya!" Talon cried, jumping up from his seat.

All eyes in the cafeteria turned to them, and Mags' face burned with shame and utter fear. Instead of sticking around, she turned and fled from the cafeteria as Onyx surged forward to try and help the other boys clean up the mess. She didn't need to look back to know that Talon was furious with her, but if she stuck around, she knew Onyx would recognise her. Hopefully, the drama of the dropped meal would be enough to stop anyone from coming to look for her.

As soon as Mags returned to the barracks, she snatched up her towel and decided to make herself scarce. Whilst the other men were still eating, she would be able to sneak into the washroom.

The events of the cafeteria played on repeat in her mind as she made her way to the showers. She paused as she stepped through the door, struck by a sense of horror at the wide hall and the showerheads scattered along each wall. There were no dividers, no privacy screens... she shuddered and looked around, hoping no one else was there.

It was bad enough that she had been coated in a full day's worth of sweat before, but now she also smelled like broth and had still-hot strings of vegetables plastered over her uniform. Without wasting time, she found a shower-head in the far corner of the space and stripped down to her underclothes. She had a spare set in her luggage and would just have to shower through them for now. The risk of getting naked was far too high.

A short time later, Mags raced out of the washroom and down the hall, wrapped in her towel as the excess water from her shorts and tank top dripped a trail on the floor behind her. She'd just reached her door when the sound of the men leaving the cafeteria echoed down to her, and she rushed inside to change into dry clothes before the boys joined her. She laid her wet underclothes on the floor beneath her bed and got into her cot, turned the light off, and laid down, pulling her blanket around her shoulders just as the others walked in.

Of course, the first thing they did was turn the light on. Mags kept her breathing slow and even and her eyes shut.

"Told ya he'd be here," Cliff muttered, walking over and prodding Mags' in the back. She let out a groan but just tugged her blanket up higher around her shoulders.

"Such an embarrassment," Shale added.

"I can't believe he dropped the soup in front of Onyx. Like... he and Talon are the best pilots there are, and all he did was embarrass us more. Talon's going to be furious in the morning," Ash said matter-of-factly.

Mags wanted to turn around and tell them all to shut up, but she heard the telltale sound of flight suit zips being opened and boots being cast aside. The knowledge that all three of the others were stripping down was enough of a horror to keep her eyes and mouth firmly shut until her pretend sleep turned into a genuine slumber.

CHAPTER
SEVEN

As if the first day of training had not been torturous enough, Talon seemed to be determined to add a new form of agony to their exercise routine every morning.

Burpees, run, combat training, run.

Burpees, run, combat training, run, more burpees.

Burpees, run, combat training, run, burpees, weight training.

Burpees, run, combat training, run, burpees, weight training, Tai Chi.

Burpees, run, combat training, run, burpees, weight training, Tai Chi, and then more blasted weight training.

To make matters worse, Talon expected them to improve each day. Their rest time started when the first person finished that exercise, which meant if you were last, you got less rest. Although Mags fell behind in the burpees, she was able to catch up during the run. Upper body weight training was an issue, but her lower body strength allowed her to keep pace. During their combat sparring, the boys had begun to break from the holds with brute strength, but she found success by avoiding them altogether.

Tai chi was the least demanding physically, but it was a real challenge to maintain concentration and balance after the previous exercises. Talon stressed that while physical and mental aptitude were important, control and balance brought everything together. There was no point in being a strong fighter if you weren't able to focus on the fight.

At the end of each day, they were expected to study the flight manual for the Fenixes and the tactics and physiology of the Hundun. Talon would quiz them during each exercise. Incorrect answers earned them extra time or repetition penalties.

After all the physical exertion, they would drag their tired bodies to dinner and then go back to their room to study. For some reason, the other three boys always decided to hit the showers together. Mags managed to find one excuse or another say she was planning to go at a different time, but night after night, every attempt she made to go to the washroom at odd or unexpected times was met by failure in the form of several naked men already in the room.

It was after one such unsuccessful attempt that she decided to head to the toilet instead. She did her best to clean herself with a washcloth at the sink, with all her clothes on, but even she knew her stink was becoming a thing of legend. She had heard the boys muttering about it the night before, so she went the extra mile to wet down her hair as well, letting the water drip down her neck before returning to her room.

Thankfully, when Mags walked back into their quarters, the other three were all sitting on their beds with their slates open, caught in deep conversation.

"Can you imagine what it was like the first time people saw these things arriving on Earth?" Shale exclaimed. He panned the paused image on his slate for their entire room to see. The footage was from an early encounter between the Airforce and the Hunduns. Back then, the human aerial military had only been made up of fighter jets. The image was grainy and slightly blurred, but it did little to detract from the hellish creature on the screen.

The Hundun were about twenty metres long and around ten metres wide. They had two pairs of membranous wings with a total wingspan of about twenty metres. They were incredibly flexible and strong, which gave them a huge advantage when moving around Earth's atmosphere. Unlike Earth-based flying animals, their bodies were muscular and thick, with an armour like carapace covering the top half of their body. In the position where a head would logically go, there was a single, thick, rounded plate that ran from the chest up to the top part of the body. It had two pairs of muscular legs and one pair of arms, each fifteen meters long with taloned claws at the ends.

Shale resumed the video, and the scene continued to play out, a battle between the first wave and Earth's initial defence force. The Hunduns could reach speeds of up to Mach 4, which meant they could outrun the missiles some of the time. They were also capable of stopping mid-flight and hovering or switching directions, meaning they could out manoeuvre any jet in pursuit. Their carapace was strong enough to resist tracer rounds but not enough to deflect a missile. When fighting at range, they launched grooved spines from a pair of orifices on either side of their headplate; they didn't have the same reach or destructive power of a missile, but what they lacked in firepower they more than made up for in speed. However, their primary mode of attack was to charge their prey, smashing them directly with the thick head-plate and finishing them off with their powerful claws.

Earth forces were no match for them.

"If you'd been around back then, I bet you would have crapped your pants." Cliff chuckled, picking a filthy sock off the floor and throwing it at Shale.

"Shut up. You probably would have run home crying to your mother," Shale retorted, swatting the sock away.

Mags ignored their immature behaviour. "It's amazing how something so large can move so fast in the air."

"Actually, there's more to that. When they first captured and studied the Hundun, scientists discovered that they produce a gravity warping field around their bodies. It allowed them to defy what we would consider the natural laws of physics," Ash explained.

"Like magic?" Cliff leaned closer to Ash.

"Not exactly. They still operate within set rules, but with the way it works, I suppose it would seem like magic," Ash answered.

"I don't care what they use, we'll kill them all the same," Cliff interjected. Shale gave him a high five.

"Anyway, what they discovered led us down the path of the Fenix program. Our technology at the time couldn't hope to match them, so instead, scientists discovered a way to create a hybrid. Cloning technology was still relatively new back then, but the threat of invasion was enough to fast track the program. Using DNA from the Hundun killed in battle, we were able to create our own version of them. Ones that weren't connected to the hive-mind; ones that we controlled using individual neural links instead."

"That's good to know, I don't like the idea of sharing my mind with another creature," Cliff muttered, seeming genuinely horrified.

I'm sure other creatures wouldn't want to share their mind with you, either, Magnolia thought to herself.

"Because the creatures don't have any individuality, it was easier for us to fashion a connection between us and the newly named Fenixes," Ash added.

"Well, I'm just glad we still get to use missiles and guns," Cliff grunted.

"Indeed, the Fenix are the perfect combination of alien physiology and human technology. We have most of their advantages and almost none of their weaknesses. The only thing we lack is numbers. For them, every creature is an effective fighting unit, but we need to be trained to fly, and our production capabilities can't match theirs."

Mags sighed. "And that's the reason why we hide."

"Well, those days are done. We're gonna kill 'em all and

take back our planet," Cliff declared with a wicked grin. He went around the room, high fiving each of them in turn. Mags return his gesture with less enthusiasm than the others.

They would need more than sheer bravado to win against the Hunduns.

A fter almost two full weeks, Talon trimmed down their physical training time and finally let them into the simulators.

"Moon Squadron! The bio interfaces in these pods are designed to fully integrate with your own bodies, just like you would with a Fenix. When you are on mission, you will not have time for a break. These pods will provide you with all the sustenance you need and resolve any waste byproducts." Talon patted a metal tank on the side of one of the sims that echoed, sounding hollow and empty.

Mags couldn't hide the disgust on her face. She'd heard about it, of course, but she wasn't keen on the idea of sitting on a hot machine full of her own piss and crap. The boys, however, high-fived each other behind her.

"Sync up." Talon gestured to the units expectantly. "I have programmed my own Fenix into the scenario with an AI pilot, and it will act as your enemy in this mission."

Now it was time to test how good Willow's hacking skills were. Normally, each pilot's unique identity was registered in a central database; it allowed the system to accurately sync the pilot to their suitable Fenix and avoid any unauthorised connections. Mags took the nearest pod and settled into it. As soon as she laid down, several connectors snaked their way toward the corresponding ports in her suit and linked up automatically. When the last port behind her neck clicked into place, a face mask lowered. The pod door closed, and she felt the neural link syncing with her mind.

This sim felt different the moment the heads-up display flashed to life in front of her, though it showed all the usual information—airspeed, altitude, attitude, armaments, and other situational data, it was far more intuitive. Cycling through the different systems and control statuses was a simple thought away. She didn't have to press a specific button anymore, her mind was now the controller. After that amazing realisation, she also felt the simulated sensation of wind flowing over her face and beneath her wings. She floated buoyantly through the air as she soared over the computer generated green patchwork of Earth. She initiated a slight right bank, and the Fenix responded immediately. The latency between her thoughts and the movements of the craft were so precise she felt like she was really flying. She looked around and could see three other craft to her left and right, which she assumed were her squadron, then, another craft blinked into existence in front of them. The AI Talon.

"Moon Squadron, welcome to the real basic training," Talon's voice sounded in Mags' head, feeling so much more real than Willow's had through a headset. *"Forget whatever you learned prior to now. The simulators that you trained on are nothing compared to what we have here. This is as close as*

you are going to get to the real thing. The simulated Fenix feels everything you feel, and you'll feel everything it does." As if on cue, she felt one of her squadron mates lightly nudge into her side, knocking her off course and into the others. It caused a chorus of grunts of disapproval.

Talon ignored it. *"Your first sortie today will be a good old-fashioned wrestle between my AI and you. The only rules are one on one. We fight until the simulator determines your Fenix can no longer continue. Let's begin."* Without warning, Talon performed a quarter turn barrel roll, flipped his craft around with surprising agility, and arrowed toward them.

He targeted Cliff first, barrelling into him with such force they shot toward the simulated ground as if they'd fallen out of the sky. The rest of the Fenixes hovered above, watching in silence as Cliff and the Hundun spun round and round. Mags used her advanced HUD display to zoom in on the action, noting that Talon's AI already had Cliff in a 'clawhold'. It was over in seconds. As soon as his Fenix dematerialised from the simulation, the AI shot back up toward them. It targeted Ash, then Shale next, both lost to the 'shoulder claw'. For Mags, though, it reserved the much hated 'mandible claw'. Even though she knew it was just a programmed AI, a part of her really thought it was on purpose.

That was just the first round. Several more followed. Although none of the boys made any progress, Mags used the same technique she'd employed on the mat; she danced around the AI each time it tried to lunge at her. Eventually it would catch her, but it took longer after every round. Each time they all lost, Talon reset the simulator.

Throughout the day, Mags was so exhausted that her mind was screaming at her to give up, but then she thought of her father and knew she couldn't. She was terrified that being back in the Fenixes would destroy the very last pieces of him. When she thought of her father, she wondered how he and the rest of her family had taken her disappearance. Would they be mad at her for what she did? Had they tried to reach out to her? She had no way to know.

After a full day of beat downs, their squadron retired to their quarters for much needed rest.

Mags was laying on her back, eyes closed, trying to ignore the million-and-one places her body was throbbing. She figured the one good thing about the training keeping her so busy was that she had little time to notice the ache in her chest caused by missing Willow and her family. She was enjoying the quiet and just about to fall asleep when Shale groaned on the cot next to hers.

"Talon's AI is a real pain in the arse."

"Don't you mean back, shoulders, and neck," Ash muttered. His cot creaked in the darkness as he was clearly trying to get comfortable.

"Listen to you wusses complain," Cliff huffed. "I got at least three hits on him."

"You mean three tiny butt pats?" Shale clarified.

Mags laughed along with the others, thinking back to how proud Cliff had been when he'd managed to tap the AI the first time, even though it had obliterated him a moment later.

"I don't think it liked you fondling its arse, given how it

smashed you afterwards," Ash said in a faux thoughtful tone.

"Well, at least I got something. What about Marsh? He just danced around, didn't even try to fight. At one point, I think it gave up on him; must be programmed to sense a loser."

Mags' jaw tightened at the insult. She might not have sparred with the AI as much as the others, but she also hadn't been defeated as much either. If they were in their real Fenixes fighting the Huns, she would have outlived all of them. She cleared her throat, deepened her voice, and muttered. "Piss off, you were just too busy getting beaten up like losers to see what I was doing."

If Talon's AI had caught up with her, she knew she wouldn't have lasted long. Talon taught them it was all about the technique and not the size, something she was still trying to master. She couldn't avoid the grapple forever, one day she would have to fight.

She contemplated a solution for their problem; they needed to stop fighting harder and focus on fighting smarter.

"We need a new strategy," she mused, tired of the unproductive insult-slinging. She hadn't left everything and everyone she loved behind to fight the Huns only to get caught up in petty battles with her squadmates.

"Oh, really?" Cliff snorted, his amusement evident in his tone. "And what would you propose, pipsqueak?"

"What if we worked together?" Her own response was as much a surprise to herself as it must have been to the others.

"Can't. The rules of engagement are clear, one on one," Ash said, always the know-it-all.

Mags rolled her eyes. "He never said we couldn't tag team."

The cot to her side creaked, and she looked over, just able to see Ash propping himself up on his elbows, his eyes catching the light as he looked over at her. "What do you mean?"

"Well, we always fight him until we lose, and then he moves on. What if, when one of us is losing, another jumps in to let them have a break? It's still one on one, but it will give us a chance to recover in between duels."

The silence was so complete she could hear the low hum of the electronics embedded in the walls around them. Then, Cliff cheered. "You sneaky bastard, that might actually work!"

The group stayed up late that night, concocting a plan for how they would signal each other and what order was best for the tag-team effort. When they finally fell asleep, they did so with a renewed sense of hope.

The next day, they started their training with much more enthusiasm. It took three rounds to properly coordinate the signal and timing, but they finally synchronised their attacks and brought the AI down.

Then, Talon reset the scenario... and they did it again.

After the third victory, the sims powered down, and the group rose from their pods to find Talon standing between them, glaring at them. "What the hell was that? The rules of engagement are clear. One-on-one combat."

"It was, sir," Ash said, unable to resist a smile.

"We never fought at the same time," Shale added.

"We fought you one-on-one," Cliff said. "We just took turns."

He looked at each of them and growled as he rounded on Mags. "Why are you so quiet, huh? Got nothing to add?" He gestured behind himself to the other boys. "I know it had to be your plan, those morons haven't got a single brain cell between them. But you... you're different. I see the way you move, the way you think. Your father was a great strategist too, my father speaks highly of him. But don't get cocky. It will get you killed." Talon turned away from her.

Mags ran a hand through her sweat-soaked hair, tearing her mind away from the mention of her father. "It won't be like that out there."

"What was that?" Talon turned back sharply. The others flinched.

"It won't be like that out there, sir." Mags slipped out of her pod and got to her feet, standing straight and proud. "The Huns aren't going to make us line up nicely to fight one-on-one. They don't care about rules of engagement. They'll kill us all the same."

Talon stared at them for the longest time before barking, "Moon Squadron, dismissed!" He turned and marched toward the door. Just before he reached it, he called out over his shoulder, "Also, Marsh... spend extra time in the shower tonight. You stink."

"Yeah." Cliff shoved Mags' shoulder. "You stink."

The other two boys laughed along and shoved past her on their way out. She let them go, face burning, as she knew they were telling the truth. Her hurried wipe downs in the restrooms were no substitute for a real shower, and even though she had become used to her own stench, there were times where she would catch an extra whiff and found it hard to resist the urge to gag on it.

CHAPTER

EIGHT

That night at dinner, Mags considered slipping out early. She would happily skip her meal if it meant time in the shower alone. However, she was pinned to her seat as the squadron reports were displayed on the wide screens. Each night, more and more teams joined the ranks of airworthy squadrons. Their stats for kills and scenarios won in the simulators kept growing. Moon Squadron's, though? Well, that was as static as their training felt.

The worst part of it all was that Talon didn't bother lecturing them. He just ate at their side, enduring the stares and whispers of the men around them. But it was impossible for Mags to ignore the way the other pilots would mutter words like, "General's son", "disgrace", and "dishonour". Talon's jaw would tighten, but he never argued. He never said anything. But of most interest to Mags, he never took it out on them. Sure, he worked them hard in training, but he never admonished them in front of the others.

Mags was considering the contradiction that was Talon as she and the others returned to their room. As usual, Shale, Ash, and Cliff grabbed their towels and toiletries.

"You coming, stinky?" Cliff asked, kicking the leg of Mag's cot as he passed.

"Later," Mags grunted, pretending to be absorbed in the tactics text she was reading on her slate.

Shale snorted. "We're never going to get our airworthy ranking," he said, playfully elbowing Cliff. "We're gonna die of suffocation thanks to Marsh's stench before then."

The three of the boys laughed as they walked out of the room, and Mags flopped back on the bed.

They were right.

As she took a deep breath in, the odour coming from her own body was so strong her eyes started to water. However, she couldn't go out now. From what she had observed, the washroom was busy from right after dinner straight through to lights out. By that point, she was fast asleep in her bed. Their days were so exhausting that staying up beyond that to sneak to the showers had been nothing more than a passing thought.

But now?

Well, she felt she had little choice.

So, instead of actually being asleep by the time the others returned, she just pretended to be.

It was difficult to stay awake. The only way Mags managed to keep her mind from drifting off was to think of

Willow. Replaying some of her favourite conversations or most adventurous game sessions was enough to keep her attention. Several times, her mind threatened to veer into more romantic territory, but it felt wrong to be imagining their shared kisses when her personal hygiene left so much to be desired.

Slowly, the sounds around Mags turned from the others complaining about Talon to Cliff's sonorous snores and Ash's sleep muttering. It was enough to make Mags grateful that Talon worked them so hard. If he didn't, she wouldn't be getting any sleep at all with that noise. Being awake to hear it also made it easier for her to keep her brain from slipping into dreams, and she opened her eyes. The small room she shared with the other three looked even smaller in the darkness. With only the cold radiance of the communication panel by the door to light the lines of the walls and ceiling, it felt almost as though she was back in her own bunk at home.

Thinking of home was a good way to pass the hours. When Mags was certain it was late enough for her to sneak out, she used her slate to check what the time was. She wound up checking it four times before she decided everyone else would be asleep by now.

Careful not to wake the others, she slipped out of bed and picked up her towel and small bag of toiletries. She had already wrapped a clean set of training clothes up and stowed them under her pillow, so they were easy to retrieve. Deciding that barefoot would be quieter than shoes, she didn't put on the slippers she kept under her bed and padded over to the door.

Outside, the corridor lighting had been dimmed to emergency reserves. It was also dead silent out there.

Well, as dead silent as things could be on a ship that was constantly buzzing or humming with some sort of critical life-support system.

The most important part was that the corridors were empty. By the lack of sound coming from the other sleeping quarters, the older pilots had retired for the night too. Even though Mags wasn't aware of what their training regimen was like, their dinners had become tense with the reports about the Hundun movement and critical life support shortages growing more dire each night. Every man, plus Mags, in the armada knew what they were fighting for. They knew that the survival of everyone and everything they held dear was dependent on them.

The mental reminder of why she had signed up was enough to wake her tired brain on her sneaky tip-toed trip to the washroom. When she reached it, she let out a soft, almost imperceptible breath of relief to find it unlocked. She wouldn't have put it beyond the various captains to try and close it off at night to ensure everyone was getting their rest.

Luckily for Mags, the inside of the washroom was just as quiet as the corridor. It was nowhere near as well lit, with only a row of flickering emergency lights down the middle of the room. It served her well, especially as she was able to disappear into the far corner and undress under the cover of shadows.

Nose wrinkling at her own odour, Mags set her clothes far away from the shower-head, and once she was certain they wouldn't get soaked, she turned the water on. A loud groan of relief slipped from her lips as it rained down over her. She shook her head at her own fascination with something as mundane as a shower.

As much as she wanted to take her time to enjoy the moment, she knew better than to test her luck. If she was caught here, there would be no hiding the fact she truly did not belong amongst the pilots. And she had a feeling discovery would be the least of her concerns if she was found by the wrong person.

With a sense of deep regret, Mags retrieved her soap and washed herself off as quickly and thoroughly as possible. She tried to console herself by making a mental promise to sneak out again to do the same thing before her stench got so bad. Even as she dried off, she felt different. Pulling on fresh clothes over her newly washed, still-warm skin felt like a slice of paradise.

Gathering up her things, Mags made her way to the door. When she opened it, she peered up and down the corridor, didn't see anything, and started making her way toward her own room.

"What do you mean you think he snuck someone into his quarters?" the voice echoed down the corridor to where Mags was standing, and she froze. It sounded familiar.

Footsteps echoed down the otherwise quiet space.

"Exactly what I said, pilot. If you weren't caught napping on guard duty, perhaps you'd know what I was talking about!" an older, far more disgruntled voice snapped.

Mags bit her lip. The voices were coming from the junction near the door to her room. She could try and make a run for it, but she wasn't sure if she would make it in time. Her only other option was to go back the way she came. The corridors in the area were all in a grid-like pattern, so it was possible she could just loop around back to her room, and whoever was coming her way might not see her.

"I apologise, sir. I will take whatever punishment you wish to assign for that. It was lax of me, and the double training duties in addition to the night-guard assignments are no excuse," the younger man said.

Mags' eyes widened as she recognised the voice.

Onyx.

The footsteps stopped, and Mags saw Onyx and another man standing just at the corner. She bit her lip as she started to backtrack, taking advantage of the way Onyx's comment had clearly outraged his elder.

The man shook his head. "Back when I was young, we worked ourselves to the bone! Your lot are always complaining about meeting rest requirements and needing mental health days. It's pitiful! We probably—"

Mags rolled her eyes as the ranting continued. She purposefully tuned out the ridiculous garbage the older man was spitting out, having no time for such rants. However, she did wince when Onyx spluttered something that drew a whole new tirade from the man.

How in the Worldship did he become one of the top pilots in his year if he didn't know to keep his mouth shut when a ranking officer was ranting?

Rounding the corner, Mags raked her eyes along the walls and took stock of her options. Unfortunately, she had stumbled right into one of the longer corridors on the level. This one, if her memory served, held the doors that led to the sleeping quarters of the various captains, as well as the large double entry doors for the cafeteria. She knew the cafeteria was a bad idea, and if Onyx and the other man were headed this way, she was unlikely to make it to the end of the corridor in time to escape their notice.

Knowing she had little choice but to hide, Mags bit her lip and looked at the door closest to her. The old, scratched off characters on it seemed to indicate it was a storage room of some type. She grabbed the manual handle on it and tugged it open, hoping it wouldn't trigger any alarms.

As the door opened, Mags instantly regretted her decision.

Sure, the door was unlocked.

And there weren't any alarms....

But it clearly wasn't a storage room.

There was a neatly made cot pushed up against one wall of the narrow space and a chest of drawers set beside it. A pilot uniform was laid over the top of the dresser. The occupant of the room was currently standing, training jumpsuit hanging loose around his sculpted torso, leaning against a woman, whose brown maintenance uniform was hanging open in all the places it needed to be for the heated kissing and grinding they were engaging in.

"Talon?" Mags spluttered, eyes almost bulging out of her head as he turned around, protectively covering the woman with him with his own body at the interruption.

"Marsh?" The growl in his voice was nothing short of terrifying.

"That's enough backtalk, Onyx! Show me where my son's room is, or I will have you charged for wasting my time."

Mags winced. In the darkness, she had been unable to identify the man who was with Onyx. But now? From his voice, she knew it was none other than General Li.

Panic, rare and fleeting, flashed over Talon's face as he turned to look at the woman he had previously been kissing.

"Quick, under the bed!" Mags hissed as she turned back, pulling the door shut and locking it from the inside.

The young woman choked out, "What?"

Talon glanced warily between Mags and the woman, but he jutted his chin toward the cot on the opposite side of the room. "Under the bed, now!" he said, voice urgent yet tender.

As the young woman scrambled to comply, Mags gestured for Talon to zip his training suit back up. If she had been the kind of person to appreciate the male form, she knew she would have just gotten a rather spectacular eyeful. As it was, she was pleased to not have the vivid reminder of what she had just walked in on in front of her. Instead, she dropped her bundle of clothes and her towel to the floor and kicked them back under the bed, feeling terrible that the poor young woman had to be under there with them. She snatched Talon's slate off the end of his bed and sat down, tapping the screen to wake it just as there was a banging on the door.

"Captain! Open this door immediately."

Talon spared Mags a glance as he took two long steps to cover the distance to the door.

"Training," Mags mimed.

After nodding, Talon opened the door.

General Li, who had been just about to knock again, froze with his fist in the air as he looked around the room. "What is the meaning of this?" he barked, some of the bite taken out of his tone by what Mags could only assume was surprise.

Mags held up the slate, her fingers trembling from the adrenaline of the last few moments. "Training," was all she said.

"Disgusting," General Li spat, pointing at his son. "You cannot train your men in the allocated time, so you try and push them up the rankings by training them secretly in the middle of the night?"

The carved lines of Talon's jaw set hard and a muscle in his neck twitched. "I worry the Hundun care not for our sleep hours. I was merely trying—"

"Silence!" General Li's voice was loud enough Mags was concerned he would wake the men in the rooms alongside Talon's. "You—" he pointed at Mags "—out. Onyx, see that this boy is returned to his room."

The general waited for Magnolia to set the slate down and walk out of the room before he entered. As he pulled the door shut behind himself, Mags caught him demanding, "Where is Lily? She was not in our apartment when I returned from—"

"Well, damn… that was close," Onyx muttered, running his hand over the fine spray of stubble coating his jaw as he led the way back to Mags' room. "What were you doing in there, Marsh?"

Mags realised that she had left her dirty clothes in the bundle she'd kicked under Talon's bed and shoved her empty hands into her pockets. "Uh… training."

It was a lie, and she had a feeling he knew it too.

Onyx shook his head as he let his hand drop. When he looked over at her, Mags quickly turned away, suddenly far more interested in the doors they were passing.

"Well, if that's gonna be your story, stick to it. Probably best not to mention what you saw in Talon's room. Or who. If you saw anyone at all."

Mags nodded and grunted, knowing they were both accepted forms of communication amongst young men her age. It seemed to be enough to satisfy Onyx as they stopped outside of her door.

"For what it's worth, I know Talon is pleased with the progress you and the others are making," Onyx said quietly.

It was enough to make Mags choke on a laugh. "Uhh… I'm not so sure about that," she replied, forcing her voice lower than she normally did when she was speaking to the others. She kept her head down, too. The lack of full lighting would make it harder for Onyx to recognise her, but even then, she didn't want to take any unnecessary chances.

"It's true. He's a hard-arse, so he won't admit it, but he has filled me in on your gains every night during our debriefs. It sounds like you are all doing your best." Onyx reached over, patting Mags' shoulder. "Did he tell you why he was saddled with the punishment of training you guys?"

"No."

Talon rarely told them anything. As much as she knew she shouldn't be eager for potential gossip, Mags found herself hovering by Onyx's side curiously.

"His father sent our squadron on a suicide mission to scout the growing Hundun swarm. We didn't realise what was going on until we were in the thick of it. The instant we had the preliminary scans, General Li privately ordered Talon to return and leave us behind to cover his exit and get more detailed surveillance… but there was a whole fleet of Hun around us, and if we'd stayed, we would have died."

Mags let out a low whistle. Sacrificing almost an entire squadron of top-of-the-line Fenixes and their highly skilled pilots seemed like a phenomenal price to pay.

"The problem is, Talon sees us as family and was horrified by his father's command. He disobeyed him and ordered us to come back with him. We were unable to get the detailed scans, and now the information we are working with is not as complete as it should be. Then, to top it off, Talon took a heck of a hit on the way back and wound up with an injury. His father, as you can expect, was furious. He still is."

Onyx sighed heavily. "The point is, don't take it too personally. If Talon seems pissed off, it's not because of you. He's had a tough time of it." Patting Mags' shoulder, Onyx added, "Just keep it up, okay? We're all fighting for something out there, and you will be able to do your part well. Don't let any of those old fools at dinner make you feel otherwise."

Mags' heart melted at the kind words from Onyx. They reminded her of something Willow might say.

It took all of her restraint to keep her mouth shut. She had a feeling asking Onyx to pass her love on to his sister would only make an already weird night that much weirder.

"Got it. Thanks," she said instead. She stepped aside and let his hand fall off her shoulder, then returned to her room.

A few minutes later, when Mags was safely tucked in her own bed, she let out of a soft breath and closed her eyes. After spending hours trying not to get to sleep, everything that had happened in the past half hour now made that seem like a luxury. She *wished* she could get to sleep, but with the way her mind was racing, she accepted the fact that she was just going to be very tired in the morning.

NINE

The next day, Talon was waiting for Mags and the others in the training room, standing in that stoic, expectant silence of his. Without a word, they started their regular training regime. Mags continued to glance over at Talon as she started her burpees, surprised that he didn't look half as tired or wary as she felt. She was torn between asking him about the previous night and hoping he said absolutely nothing about it.

Any hope of being able to focus on her burpees and forget about the awkward mess of the dark hours disappeared when Mags made the mistake of looking up. Talon was watching her, and before she could look somewhere else, he crooked his finger at her and stepped away from the others.

Holding back a sigh of apprehension, Mags stopped her sequence of burpees and walked over to join her captain. He turned his back away from the other three boys who were now watching with undisguised interest as they puffed their way through the exercises.

"You left your clothes in my room last night," Talon said in a low voice, gesturing to a bulbous bag of cloth near the door of the exercise training area. "I took them to the laundry and had them cleaned for you."

Mags blinked. She wasn't sure exactly what she was supposed to say to that. So, she just muttered, "Uh, thanks."

"I am guessing you were up late to shower, judging by the smell of you," Talon said, eyeing her as he stepped closer.

Mags resisted the urge to step back.

"I'm not going to ask why you showered at that time, well after curfew. We all have our own pasts, and I have a feeling whatever you experienced in yours is causing you to act strangely now," Talon explained, voice still whisper quiet.

He wasn't really hitting the target, but he was close enough that Mags didn't argue. She just nodded.

"I am curious though, why my room?"

"I saw General Li and Onyx coming and panicked. I turned and ran. I thought your room was a storage closet," Mags replied, whispering also and trying to ignore the growing curiosity in the eyes of her squadmates.

"Ah." Talon pressed his lips together, and the solid set of his shoulders sagged just the slightest. "That is because it is a storage closet. Well, it was. With the draft, they had to reassign the function of many rooms."

Mags found it interesting that the General's own son

had been relegated to a decrepit storage cabinet, but she kept the thought to herself. The more she talked, the longer the conversation would be. As much as she enjoyed learning new information, every word she spoke to Talon risked revealing the truth about her identity.

"And that woman... Lily... She's my wife," Talon said. The way he leaned forward and looked into her eyes told Mags that this was what the conversation was really about.

Mags thought back to the flashes she got of the pretty woman Talon had been kissing, pinned up against the wall of his room. She hadn't really been able to see much beyond, well... she'd seen a fair bit. But what stuck in her mind the most was the fact she was wearing a brown uniform.

"She's in maintenance?" Mags blurted before she could stop herself. She clenched her teeth as Talon stiffened.

What was the son of the Great General Li doing with a maintenance worker? Mags herself believed that maintenance was one of the most critical jobs on the Worldship Honour, as none of the inhabitants would survive in squalid or broken living conditions. However, their society saw it differently, and maintenance was the lowest of the low positions one could find themselves in.

"She is," Talon confirmed, a defensive edge to his voice. "We have been together since we were fourteen. We were lucky to be put together in the draft, but my family does not approve. With me gone, they are watching her closely. Just like everyone else, I do not have leave to return to her during this time. But I had to see her. I needed a reminder of—"

"Of what you're fighting for?" Mags said, cutting him off.

Unlike all of the other times Talon had been interrupted where he had grown angry, this time, he just nodded.

Part of Mags was relieved that she had not walked in on him cheating on his wife. Even though she would have kept the secret, it would have felt all kinds of wrong. But... a man trying to spend time with the woman he loved before he marched toward likely death? That, Mags could understand.

The thought made her yearn to see Willow.

"Don't worry, your secret is safe with me. We all have someone we're fighting for," Mags said softly.

Talon's almost ever-present frown softened for just a moment, and Mags smiled back at him. "Good. I'm glad you understand. I didn't want to have to punish you for being out of your room late."

And just like that, the jerk version of Talon was back in full force.

The captain stood up and crossed his good arm over his sling. "Now, get back to your routine before I give you fifty extra burpees."

"Yes, Captain," Mags said, rolling her eyes as she turned and jogged back to her spot on the mat.

The rest of the training session went well, and it was becoming clear that not only were the Moon Squadron complaining less about the physical exertion, but they were also getting better at it. Just before they were about to suit up for their simulator, Talon stopped them by clearing his throat and holding his hand up.

"Moon Squadron, I was pleasantly surprised with your tactics yesterday. As such, we will be moving on to weapons training today."

There was a cheer from the others, and a round of high-fives that they included Mags in. She was less than enthused by having to clap her hands against their sweaty ones, but she hoped it was a good sign that they didn't hate her anymore. It was also confirmation of what Onyx had told her the night before, and she wondered if her run-in with Talon and Lily had made him open up a bit.

Talon continued, "As we've discussed, the munitions on your Fenix are limited. Pick the wrong targets, and you'll be overwhelmed in melee combat, or even worse— hitting your own allies. You'll need to make every shot count."

This time when Talon got them set up in the sim, he added AI Hunduns into the scenario. There were so many, more than they had missiles.

They spent days trying to fight the simulation, to beat it, but all they got was body pain and headaches at the end of the day as they went through the neural feedback of their ships dying again, and again, and again.

At the end of their fourth day of munitions training, the group retired to their sleeping quarters, the vibe between them more dejected than it had been before. Not only were they tired and not progressing, but the date of the final mission was barrelling closer. Whenever they failed, all

Mags could do was think about Willow and her family, about how if they failed for real, the people she loved the most would die within weeks.

Shale groaned as he flopped back onto his bed. "This is impossible, there's no way we can hit that many targets with only four missiles. There's just too many. Even on my best run, I still had twenty to get through."

"I can barely hit more than two targets with one missile. Once, when I thought I had ten of them lined up, just as I fired, they scattered," Ash muttered, unzipping his flight suit and shaking his head.

"I don't get it, either." Shale kicked off his boots. One of them hit Cliff, who turned and raised a fist in warning.

The room went silent. Mags knew they were waiting for her to chime in. Ever since her success with the tag-team idea, she had become somewhat of an advisor. "I've been thinking about it," she admitted. "We keep chasing them, so we're always one step behind. All they need to do is keep us running circles around ourselves until we die. Instead of just following them, we need to anticipate what they will be doing."

"Do you have some kind of precognitive powers you didn't tell us about?" Shale scoffed. The others laughed.

"No, idiot." Mags rolled her eyes. "Think about it; every time we aim at them, they run, we miss. We need to stop thinking about where they *are* and figure out where they are *going to be*."

"Oh... that is clever!" Ash perked up, his eyes shining in the low light of their room. "So, we pretend to aim in one place, let them run, then shoot where they're running to?"

"Exactly!" Mags grinned.

"Ah, I get it." Cliff sounded approving as he laid back down on his bed. "It might even work."

The next day they enacted their plan. It wasn't easy to pull off though, as they needed to study the Hunduns' evasive tactics in greater detail. Just before the end of the day, Ash managed to nail the feint, and he blasted no less than ten Huns out of the sky with one missile. Soon after, he did it again, until only three lonely targets made it to him. He'd still lost, but it was the closest anybody had gotten.

His success spurred the rest of them on, and eventually they were able to get the massive group down to a manageable size; one they could actually defeat. When they exited the sim, Talon eyed Mags with a knowing expression.

"Moon Squadron, dismissed."

The lack of critique was enough for Mags to know Talon was pleased.

The following morning, after their physical training, Talon took them to the briefing room for the first time, where there was a large round table with several chairs around it, in the centre was a holographic display depicting several Fenixes floating above the surface.

"Moon Squadron, I think you've learned the basics of combat, but combat is more than just punching and shooting your way through. As I said before, the Hunduns have numbers on their side, so we need to be smart when we are fighting them. The formation of our squadrons and how we move around matters; you need to know where your squadron mates are at all times so you can support them or not accidentally hit them while you're out there.

"For the next week, you will study every formation we have on record. You will learn their strengths and weaknesses. And at the end of this exercise, I will pick a leader. That man will decide which one to use for any given situation. Is that clear?"

"Sir, yes, sir!"

Despite how much the others complained about the tactics training, Mags found herself excited by it. Talon was right. They had to be smart. As she spent the whole first day going through the different scenarios and formulations, she found herself wishing she had Willow there with her. When they'd been at school, they would get together to study and quiz each other into the obscenely early hours of the morning.

Still, over the next week, Mags and the guys soon learned that mental work could be just as tiring as the intense physical work. Especially when Talon still insisted on continuing the physical training.

It was several nights after the initiation of the training that Mags had her slate on her lap before she fell asleep. She had her messaging app open and, just like she had for the past few nights, she had Willow's name in the 'To' field. Her fingers hovered over the message input box, and she wondered again whether anyone would be monitoring hers or Willow's communications closely enough to see it.

The training had kept Mags busy enough that she barely had time to think about her family and Willow, but there was no way to ignore the gnawing pit in her heart that grew wider and wider by the day. It had become harder to sleep as she worried about them. The only saving grace was the knowledge that if those in charge knew of her deception, they would have come down on her already.

That gave her enough confidence to tap the message box. She typed out several different messages, then deleted them all. She did this again and again until she let out a frustrated grunt and just typed in:

Xx

Just as she was about to send it, the slate was snatched from her hand.

"What's this?" Cliff crooned, dancing out of her reach as she jumped out of bed and charged at him. "Oooh, boys! Marsh is sending a kiss-kiss to someone... to a—"

Before Cliff could read Willow's name, Mags launched at him but used a feint similar to the ones they had used in the Fenixes. She managed to elbow him in the gut and snatch the slate from him while he caught his breath. She quickly hit send and locked the slate before the others could stop her. However, Ash and Shale were more interested in laughing at their antics.

"So, a love letter, hey?" Shale asked when he had recovered from his amusement. "We didn't get our marriage assignments before we got conscripted. Don't tell me you did."

Mags pressed her lips shut, not wanting to give anything away. Her cheeks reddened of their own accord, though, and she could feel the heat rising in them as surely as the others could see it.

"Damn… Not an assignment, boys. I think our Marsh is in loooove." Cliff thumped Mags on the back before she flopped onto her bed. "C'mon. Spill the tea. Who is she?"

"No one."

A chorus of *oooooh*'s came from the others.

"Don't let her hear you say that. Women don't like it when you call them no one," Ash tutted.

"And how would you know what women like?" Mags snapped.

"What, like you do?" Ash glared at her, chin raised with indignance.

Way more than you can even imagine, Mags thought. As much as she wanted to say it, she kept her mouth shut.

"At least tell us if she's pretty," Shale said, leaning forward and resting his elbows on his knees.

Mags rolled her eyes. "Because that's the only important thing about a woman, huh? You're disgusting."

Turning and kicking the bottom of the bed so Cliff yelped and jumped off it, Mags chose to ignore them. She sat down and pulled her covers up, hoping that was the end of the conversation.

"What is the most important thing, then?" Ash asked. "Does she have nice eyes?" As much as he tried to make his tone sound like banter, there was a hint of genuine curiosity behind it.

"Does she love you for your strength?" Cliff asked, flexing his muscles and making the other two snort with amusement.

Shale perked up. "Maybe she cooks well!"

"She's clever," Mags blurted, annoyed at their implications.

"Clever?" Cliff sounded more dubious than ever.

Mags ignored him. "Yes. She's also determined. She speaks her mind. She's always been my best friend, and now—" She paused when she noticed the three young men watching her with a mix of doubt and awe.

"And now?"

"Nothing." Mags turned her back to them. "That's all you're getting. Good night."

She laid down on her pillow and pulled her blankets up high. The image of Willow taunted her as she closed her eyes, and her heart ached even more.

Just as she was falling asleep, she heard Ash whisper to the others, "Well, she sounds like a girl worth fighting for."

TEN

The next few days dragged on the same way. Every night, Mags and the others went to dinner only to find that a whole new group of squadrons had been added to the list of airworthy fighters. With each meal that passed, Mags could see the tension growing in Talon's posture, and she wondered if he hated the fact he was saddled with them. Even if, by some ridiculous twist of fate, they were all prodigies, they were all also beginners. His father had to know what he was doing by putting his son with a group of complete rookies. It made Mags feel terrible for her captain, and for the woman who he was being kept away from.

"We'll be on that list soon," Shale said, setting his drink down and grinning at the others. "I think we're doing well to get the formations down."

"Well, most of us," Cliff muttered over his noodles, eyeing Marsh.

"I'll be the judge of that," Talon said, his voice cutting

through their conversation like a knife. There was a look in his eyes that made all of the young men return to their meals. They had gotten used to his moods, and the broody darkness on his face was not the kind of vibe they messed with. "I hope you all use tonight to study. I am planning to test you on your formations over the next couple of days."

That was the exact moment that General Li appeared in the room to go over the latest additions to the airworthy list. If Talon's comment hadn't killed their moods, the fact that the Moon Squadron was still right down at the bottom of the list would have.

"Maybe the problem is we've been doing too much study," Cliff muttered to Shale, who hummed with agreement.

Talon shot them both a withering glare.

When General Li's announcement was over, the group finished their meal in silence. Talon excused himself to go over to where Onyx and his usual squadron were eating. Even though Talon never really perked up, per se, Mags couldn't help but notice how he seemed so much lighter around them. After what Onyx told her about how things were between Talon and his father, it made sense to her. The Moon Squadron was a punishment for him, and if she were in the same position, she would probably resent them too.

"He was extra uptight tonight. Wonder who twisted his boxers into a knot," Cliff said, looking over at their captain.

"You know that we're not the only ones who aren't

allowed any leisure time, right?" Mags said before she could stop herself.

Ash swallowed the noodles he had just shoved into his mouth. "What do you mean?"

"So long as we aren't on that list, he doesn't get to go out or see his family either. It's not just us who could do with a break." She sighed as she stacked her teacup in her noodle bowl.

"That isn't healthy," Shale said, shaking his head. "For any of us."

"It isn't, but what on this ship really is?" Mags shrugged as she got to her feet. "I'm going to head back to our room and study."

She exited the dining room, thoroughly aware that her squadmates were whispering behind her back. They were all exhausted, she understood that, but sitting at their table and whining about it wouldn't fix it.

The other boys joined Mags after half an hour. They all grabbed their clothes and towels and went to the bathroom to clean up. When they returned, they all sat down and studied in silence. It was odd. They were rarely able to put their banter aside and just get down to business, but Mags appreciated it.

Hours dragged by, and her eyes grew gritty. Finally, she set her slate down on her lap and leaned back against the wall beside her cot. She was just about to turn the device off, when a message pinged onto the screen.

Hey, sorry it's taken me a while to respond to your message. I wanted to make sure our encryption was perfect before risking a reply… I miss you. Xx

Mags' heart skipped a beat. She hadn't been expecting to hear back from Willow, but seeing that message and knowing she was awake at the same time…

Ash looked up from his own slate. "What is it?"

Jumping at the sudden question, Mags hurried to find an answer. Any answer. "I, uh… just saw the time. It's really late. We've got to get to bed." Mags slipped off her bed, grabbed her bag of toiletries, and shoved her slate into it. It was well after curfew, so the shower room would be closed, but she would still have access to the restroom. She could use the sink in there to brush her teeth… and the privacy to send a message to Willow.

Shale perked up. "Late enough to get to bed, eh?"

Immediately, Mags was wary. His tone was anything other than sleepy or compliant.

Rolling his shoulders and grinning, Cliff said, "Late enough to get to bed, but the night is still young. Why don't you boys get dressed, and we can go and see what's happening in other parts of the ship. Sleep is for rookies. We might not have our airworthy sign-offs yet, but if we spend another night without some form of recreation, we're going to lose our minds."

Mags had never heard a more ridiculous idea before in her life. Sneaking out could put everything they were working toward at risk. "You three are ridiculous. You're going to get caught." Before they could argue, Mags strode out of the room.

The corridors outside were empty. Mags made her way to the restroom and immediately locked herself in one of the toilet stalls. She pulled her slate out and unlocked it before typing a message.

> It's so good to hear from you. I've missed you too. So much. The company here is just about as bad as the smell. I never have that problem when I'm with you.

After hitting send, Mags stared at the screen of the new chat log she now shared with Willow. She wondered if Willow had packed her slate up for the night, but then the little rippling string of dots at the bottom of the screen indicated that she was typing.

> I'm glad to see they haven't trained the sense of humour out of you. How's training?

Mags snorted a laugh, then quickly covered her mouth with her hand as she realised she wouldn't be laughing if she was just in the stall doing a crap. She had to be more careful. Letting out a slow breath, she lowered her hand and typed.

> I wish that was a joke…

Training is hard, but I am learning a lot. I haven't thought about anything other than Fenixes for so long, and I think my mind is shutting down.

Sounds like you could use a break. Are you able to get any time off?

No. Not until the squad is deemed airworthy. Given that the idiots I'm in a squad with are planning to sneak out tonight, that could be a while.

You should go with them.

Eyebrows knitting together, Mags shook her head. The whole ship was going mad.

The only thing I want is one last chance to spend time with you before the final battle. If we sneak out now, we could ruin that. I can't risk it. We need to be on our best behaviour.

The dots on the bottom of the page rippled for far too long. Mags had just started wondering whether Willow had fallen asleep at her screen (it wouldn't be the first time), when a message finally came through.

Go. I'll take care of the security footage. I'm going to be up for a while doing other stuff anyway. Please go. There is no sense in making it to the end of training if you're too burnt out to think straight. Besides, if these guys are your squadmates, being in their good graces could save your arse. An arse which I am highly invested in, by the way. If you don't do it for yourself, do it for me.

Mags let out a low whistle. That was a low blow. She ran a hand through her short, cropped hair and tapped her foot on the floor.

Fine. You win. I'll go.

She tapped send, then realised that her words were far too snappy. She added:

Thank you. I love you.

After shoving her slate back in her toiletries bag, Mags exited the stall and decided to go over and brush her teeth anyway. Despite her reservations, the idea that she may be able to leave the restricted set of tunnels and rooms she had been confined to was exhilarating.

When she got back to the room, Shale, Cliff, and Ash were standing in their uniforms, matching grins on their faces.

"Please tell me the reason you took so long to crap was

because you were changing your mind," Shale said, bouncing from foot to foot with anticipation.

For a moment, an unhinged part of Mags found it endearing. She threw her toiletries bag onto the bed and sighed. "If we get caught, you three are dead," she said.

The others danced and pumped their fists into the air. They would have cheered too, probably, had it not been so late.

Even though she still thought it was a terrible idea, Mags smiled too.

"Come on, get back in your uniform. The ladies love a man in uniform," Ash said, hustling over and holding out Mags' flight suit.

She frowned as she took it. "Oh yeah, how would you know?"

That was enough to have the three guys laughing and shoving each other as she quickly turned her back to them and changed into her flight suit. Even though it had all of the wires running through it, they were thin enough that it was still comfortable to wear outside of training. Mags finished zipping it up and turned around to look at the others. "So... where are we going?"

ELEVEN

They heard the throbbing music well before they turned into the corridor that led to *Tian*, one of the few nightly party venues on the *Honour*. Inside, the roar of the electronic track was deafening. The bass backing was so loud that Mags swore she could feel it pulsing in her throat. She swallowed as she peered around in the darkness. The wide dancefloor was lit by a rainbow of intermittent, flashing strobes. Each flicker of the lights revealed a tightly packed space, with bodies writhing and grinding together.

A hand squeezed Mags' shoulder and she jumped as she turned to see Shale leaning in closer. "Pick your jaw up off the floor! You look like you've never seen a club before."

In all fairness, Mags *hadn't* seen one before. Given how recent her eighteenth birthday was, and how she would have far preferred to spend time gaming with Willow, going to a club was never on the list of things she wanted to do. Being here now, though, she supposed she could see the allure. Letting go and indulging in dancing and sweating, she was sure it would be easy to lose oneself in the escape of it all.

Coming up to stand on her other side, Shale elbowed her in the ribs. "Come on. Let's get on the floor. We'll never get the ladies if we stand here all night."

Mags finally shut her mouth and gulped.

Get the ladies?

She rolled her eyes. Of course that was their goal.

Peering around, she noticed that there seemed to be a fairly even spread of men and women on the floor. For the most part, people had already split off into couples, but there were some groups scattered across the space as well. Mags followed the others onto the edge of the floor and had to stop herself from choking as they started to dance.

Suddenly, she realised the boys might have had a better chance of getting the ladies if they did indeed stand on the edge of the dancefloor. What they were doing now was nothing more than crude gyrating.

Mags had never enjoyed the dancing classes she had been forced to endure growing up, but even she could move better than Cliff, Shale, and Ash.

She was about to prove it when she remembered *who* she was supposed to be.

There was no way that *Marsh* would be able to master the elegant hand movements and hypnotising hip sways of the dance skills *Mags* was taught as a child. However, with the way the others were staring at her, she had to start dancing before they got suspicious. So... with a great deal of self-loathing, she started pumping her fists and her pelvis like they were.

Several songs went by before the group was approached by a woman wearing a skin-tight dress that seemed to be made from a repurposed set of medical scrubs. Despite the previous function of the fabric, she had cinched it in just right and cut a neckline daring enough that Mags doubted the others noticed what the dress was made of. She made her way to Shale and lured him away by taking his hands.

Mags couldn't believe it. She wasn't sure what the woman was attracted to, but she knew it had *nothing* to do with Shale's dancing.

Ash leaned in. "It's the uniform, I swear." Then he punched Mag's shoulder and jutted his chin to a group of women in the distance, watching them from a bar that was serving a range of refreshments. "See! Told you."

Cheeks heating with the way the women were looking at them, Mags quickly turned away.

"Yeah, play it cool!" Cliff shouted, playfully shoving Mags. She shook her head and tried to catch her breath as she made her dance movements less, well... just *less*.

The other two laughed and shook their heads at her, but they resumed their gyrating all the same. Mags sincerely hoped that the ladies at the bar took the hint and looked at someone else for a while. However, when Cliff's eyes grew wide, she only had a moment to realise what was happening before a gentle hand settled on her shoulder.

Jumping at the contact, Mags spun around. She was

just about to tell the woman who had approached her that she wasn't interested in a dance when she saw who it was.

"Willow?"

Mags' eyes just about popped out of their sockets as she was face to face with her best friend, and the woman she loved.

Willow's eyes flashed a dizzying array of colours as the strobe lights played over her porcelain skin, and Mags gulped. She looked Willow up and down, noticing the fact that she was wearing a short, skin-tight dress that she must have taken from someone else's closet. The deep red fabric had a cling to it that made Mags' heart skip a beat.

"What are you doing here?" Mags asked.

Tilting her head to the side, Willow tapped her ear and mimed something.

Of course. The music was too loud for her to hear. Before Mags could ask again, Willow used the soft hand on her shoulder to pull her closer, and then Mags almost melted as she felt Willow's lips brushing her earlobe.

"I figured I could use a break, too."

The sound of Willow's voice and the hot brush of her breath on Mags' skin made for a dizzying combination. Still, Mags frowned. "Is this safe?" She felt like she had to shout to be heard over the din, even at such an intimate proximity.

"I've got a deep-fake algorithm running... we'll be fine." Mags was about to tell Willow to go back to her room, when Willow playfully nipped at her earlobe. "Dance with me."

A chill ran through Mags' entire body, and she was

grateful for the fact that the music drowned out the choked groan that spluttered from her.

All too aware that she was with company, Mags looked back over her shoulder.

Both Ash and Cliff were gawking at her. Their wide eyes and open mouths told her enough to know that they were as shocked as she was, albeit for different reasons. She was about to ask if they would mind if she left, but Shale gave her a double thumbs up, mouthing "Go!"

With a laugh, Mags returned her attention to Willow to find her friend smirking. Willow cocked an eyebrow at her, as if to say, *"So?"*

Mags slipped her hand into Willow's and knitted their fingers together. She then dragged her deeper onto the floor, weaving their way through the undulating mass of bodies to find a place on the floor that was away from the others and all their own. Willow didn't hesitate to wrap her arms around Mags' shoulders and step in close. Mags could feel each and every curve of Willow's body as she pressed it against hers, and she closed her eyes as she brushed her cheek against Willow's.

Even with the veritable myriad of body washes, deodorants, perfumes, and bodily scents wafting through the space, Mags took a deep breath and identified that delicious aroma that was uniquely Willow. Her knees weakened, so she draped her arms around Willow's waist and let her fingers press tightly against the sleek red fabric of her dress.

"I can't believe you're here," Mags said, pressing a kiss on Willow's cheek.

Willow pulled back just enough to rest her forehead on Mags'. "I can't either... but I'm so glad I am." As she spoke, Willow's lips brushed against Mags'.

As much as Mags enjoyed being on the dancefloor with her, she actually wished they were somewhere else. Somewhere more... private.

However, if they were somewhere private, Mags would have no excuse to keep Willow's body pulled tight against hers.

"I thought it'd be good for both of us to remember what you're fighting for," Willow said.

Then Mags kissed her.

Not a single person around them paused their own dance to look. No one pulled a face or turned away in disgust. All they saw was someone they thought was a young man kissing a young woman, and they just accepted it.

For the first time in her life, Mags finally felt *free*.

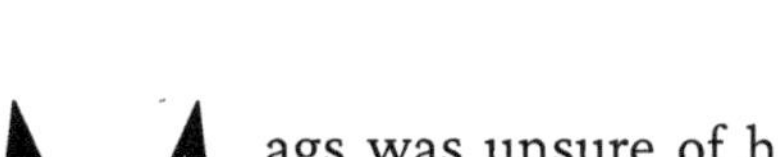

Mags was unsure of how long she was on the dancefloor for. All she knew was the feel of Willow's hands roaming over her body and the taste of her lips. The setting made Mags daring, and she slid one hand up between Willow's shoulder blade and the other below her lower back. She tilted her head to change up the angle of her kiss and was able to deepen it in a way that made Willow moan into her mouth.

If the night lasted forever, it would have not been long enough for Mags.

However, the intimate dance with Willow came to an end as Mags noticed Cliff, Ash, and Shale making their way over to her. Their faces were lit with exhilaration, even though their postures seemed to sag as they slipped through the crowd. Mags reluctantly stepped back from Willow, peeling their bodies apart and stepping around her girlfriend to shield her from the view of her squadmates.

When Cliff leaned in, there was an odd bitterness on his breath that Mags remembered from times when she'd woken in the early hours of the morning and found her father drinking moonshine. Her eyes widened. Surely, he wouldn't have had something to drink? Moonshine had been outlawed on the *Honour* for close to ninety years.

"Marsh, how's it going?" Cliff asked, voice slurring.

Yep, Mags thought to herself, *he is definitely drunk.*

Mags turned back to face Willow, and some of the twinkling in her eyes faded as she nodded. She leaned in close to Mags, pressing a gentle kiss against her cheek and whispering, "Go. Stay safe. I love you."

"I love you too," Mags replied without hesitation, even though she wasn't ready to go.

Deciding that she had to make an exit before she did something stupid, Mags stepped back and let her eyes drink in the sight of Willow in that dress, pretty hair mussed and lips plump from all the kissing, and gave her a final smile. Then, she turned around and followed the others out of the club.

It wasn't until they were a good four tunnels away that Shale turned, walking backward as he gawked at Mags. "Damn, Marsh... I thought you and that woman were going to go all the way there on the dance floor!"

Mags, who had been replaying the night in her mind, frowned as her squadmate tore her from her fantasies. If she was completely honest with herself, she had been dreaming about doing exactly what Shale was teasing her for.

"Crap, look at how much he's blushing!" Ash teased, pointing at her.

"Guess you're gonna have to message that girl of yours and tell her you found yourself a real woman," Cliff said with a guffaw that made Mags want to punch him.

"She *is* the woman I was messaging," Mags snapped back, her brain still too addled with lust to fully process that it was probably a bad idea.

The three boys cheered and whooped, shoving each other like a pack of fools.

Then, Cliff lumbered over and slung his heavy arm around Mags' shoulders. She staggered at the unexpected weight. "Marsh, my friend, she is hottttt."

Mags shoved him off. "Shut up, idiot. You're drunk."

"No, he's right. She is stunning," Shale said matter-of-factly. "I'd happily show her my strength and discipline alllll night long."

As much as Mags wanted to tell him that he had no discipline, she ignored him instead. She knew that returning the banter only prolonged conversations in these situations.

The boys fell silent for the next few metres, but before they turned into the corridors that led to the rear of the ship, Mags heard Ash mutter to himself, "I don't care what she looks like... I wish I was lucky enough to have someone that looked at me the way she looked at you."

Despite everything the others had said... despite the gaping pain in her chest at having to leave Willow behind... Mags smiled to herself at Ash's comment.

He was right.

She was lucky.

TWELVE

The next morning, Mags and the others didn't wake up until Talon barged into their room and tore their blankets off them.

"Why are you lousy idiots still asleep? Get up! If you're not in the training room in five minutes, you're all on latrine duty!"

Then, Talon was gone.

Mags groaned as she looked at the time on her slate and realised they had all not only missed their alarms but slept fifteen minutes into training time. With a sigh, she guessed that was bound to happen given the fact they got back to their room at four in the morning.

With a yawn, and kicking Shale in the backside to make sure he got up, Mags forced herself to get ready for the day. By the time she and the others stumbled onto the training mat, she was yet to successfully blink the grit out of her eyes. Every time she tried to rub them, the lights in her mind flashed and strobed in a way that reminded her of the club, and her body reacted to the memory of being so up close and personal with Willow. It was such a terrible distraction that she decided it was safer to live with the bleariness.

When Talon asked why they were all so tired, Ash made up some lie about staying up late to study formations. It was a bad choice, because he then promised to test them on exactly that after a double set of morning exercise.

After the gruelling exercise regime, Mags was awake enough to appreciate the fact she was then able to slump onto the seat of the sim console. She yawned as she fired the system up and pulled her helmet on.

Even though she didn't have trouble picking the right formation for the situation, the group all had difficulty communicating well enough to make the arrangements work without collisions. They had just gotten the hang of it when Talon threw in some other automated squadrons to make their job even harder.

Mags was still having trouble getting the formations right. She was so used to flying alone that she found it hard to remember the location of the others and then adjust their calls based on three-dimensional space. The others found their own unique ways to remember; Shale made up a weird rhyme that he recited every night, Ash drew pictures of animals to represent each one. Even Cliff, who hated everything apart from firing his weapons, managed to get the hang of it. The next day would be their final test, everything they had learned would be thrown at them in one mission.

Later that day, when training was finally over, Mags

flopped back in her bed. The fatigue made her head spin even though she was stationary, and all she wanted was to ignore everything else and just be with Willow. Despite all of the effort they had put in, her day of formation training had been ruled a complete failure by Talon, and he had warned her that if she didn't pick up her game, she would be in trouble.

Mags closed her eyes and refused to engage with the others as she mentally prepared herself for failure. She should have known the euphoria of the previous night was too good to last. What would her family think if she returned home now, rejected on the very last day? Her only consolation was nobody knew she wasn't a man. The rest of her squadron were psyching each other up and saying they were fighting for their families and for the women they had danced with the previous night.

"What's up, Marsh?"

Mags jumped as Cliff threw himself onto her cot and scared her half to death.

"Just thinking about tomorrow."

"Hey, there's nothing to worry about, we've made it this far. Nothing is going to stop us."

"Maybe for you. I'm still running into all of you during formation setup."

"Yeah, but you always know which one to call out."

As nice as the reassurance was, Mags shook her head. "That means crap if I crash into someone and kill us all."

"Don't worry about it." Shale joined them on the bed. "We're in this together, we've got this. If we fail, we'll all go down together."

"Speak for yourselves, I'm leaving you all behind," Cliff joked.

"You wouldn't!" Shale narrowed his eyes at the other young man.

There was a long silence as the two stared each other down.

Cliff finally broke. "Nah, you idiots would cry like babies if I left you." He punched Shale playfully on the arm.

"Don't worry, Marsh, we've got you covered for tomorrow. Trust us." Ash winked at Mags in a way that made her instantly wary.

"What do you mean?"

"Don't think about it too much, pipsqueak, just stick to what you're good at, and we'll take care of the rest." Cliff punched her on the shoulder this time, by this point she was so used to it she didn't even flinch anymore.

"Let him get some rest. We need Marsh to be fresh in the morning, he's in charge of all the plays, remember," Shale reminded them.

They all got off her bed and went back to their own. She was curious about what they intended to do, were they planning on pushing her out of the fight early? It would make sense, at this point she was more of a liability than assistance. She tried to figure out what their plot was, but she was so exhausted she fell asleep in the space between one thought and another.

The next day, Talon excused them from their morning exercise regime.

"This is it, gents. Your final exam. Some of you will continue as enlisted soldiers of the Honor Guard, the finest

Armada in all of humanity. The others? Well, you will bring dishonour on your entire family, shame on all humankind, and disappoint me—"

Before Talon could finish, a klaxon alert rang through the training room. The lighting shifted to flashing red, and they all froze.

"Attention all units. Report to battle stations immediately. Critical mass of Hunduns detected. Final Mission imminent. Repeat: Report to battle stations immediately."

Suddenly, Mags felt sick.

"We can't r-report to battle stations," Ash stammered, shaking his head. "We haven't finished our training."

"We are supposed to have a few more days before the fight!" Shale said.

"We haven't done our final test, yet!" Cliff added, looking beseechingly at Talon.

Talon's featured hardened, the carved lines of his face suddenly as unforgiving as they were handsome. "Moon Squadron! Consider this your new final test."

Then, without giving them a chance to argue, he turned on his heel and marched toward the exit. Mags and the boys were forced to scramble after.

When they arrived at the Fenix hangar, it was a flurry of chaos. The bird-like ships were currently hooked up to advanced monitoring systems, the cables draped all around them almost like nets. Technicians in the grey engineering jumpsuits frantically ran around them, completing the final pre-flight checks.

Talon pointed to a row of Fenixes toward the rear of the hangar, farthest away from the launch bay. "Moon

Squadron, those are your birds. Normally, we would be going over pre-flight checks together. Given the nature of the situation, we will need to rely on our engineers to do that while we get locked into the pods. You've never done pre-flight checks before, so you wouldn't really know what to look for anyway."

Talon resumed walking before they could ask any questions. He marched them past the rows and rows of Fenixes, toward a door on the far side of the Fenix Hangar and into a place that Mags had never been before.

Unlike the Fenix hangar where their ships sat, waiting and lifeless, the pod hangar was the place that brought everything to life. None of them could do any damage walking amongst their biomechanical vehicles, as they were inoperable without the pilot being connected to the pods... but in here? This was where it all happened. It was where rookies became real pilots.

Mags struggled to follow the others through the steady stream of men rushing between pods. Talon led them all the way to the rear to a set of pods against the back wall. He looked over at them, tapping four in quick succession and gesturing for them to get in.

"Moon Squadron! I know your training has been cut short, but no amount of simulator time can adequately prepare anyone for a real neural link and Fenix flight," he told them. "That said, remember your training. Remember your tactics. Do the best you can to fight with strength and discipline, and I hope to see you all on the other side." He gave them a final salute, and they responded with ones of their own.

It felt like a short pep talk given everything they had been through together, and all they might be about to face, but as men filtered into the pods and locked themselves in, they didn't have time to linger. So, they got into the pods.

Mags found that her hands were shaking as the automated cables connected to her suit ports. She let out a long, steady breath before trying again. Once she was in, she closed the pod behind herself, and it flared to life.

If going from the analogue simulator to the training simulator was a big jump, integrating into the combat pod was a giant leap. Now, Mags wasn't just lying in a pod using her thoughts to translate actions, she *was* the Fenix; mighty and strong. She could feel the weight of the plated armour around her body and wings, the weaponry attached to her torso, and the rail guns affixed to her side. Everything felt solid and firm. The display system worked much the same way as before, but this time when she began her before take-off checks as each system booted up, she felt the physical whirring and vibration of machinery around her body. She flexed her legs and arms, and the Fenix moved in the launch bay, too. After completing her final checks, Mags and the rest of the Moon Squadron requested permission to depart.

As soon as they were granted clearance, they made their way to the launch bay exit, spread their wings, and flew.

An unexpected surge of exhilaration and awe filled Mags as she held her wings wide and joined the mass exodus of ships departing the *Honour*. As she surged toward Earth's atmosphere, she felt the heat of entry scalding her feathers.

The added sensations and thrill of it reminded Mags of the very real danger she was in. Anything that happened to her Fenix would translate back to her on the ship. The buffer was gone. There was no safety net.

Luckily for the humans, they had General Li leading the armada. Mags might not have liked what she heard about him, or how he treated Talon, but Li's record of service spoke of an unparalleled successful career. He was gruff and curt in all things, but also highly efficient. As he ordered the fleet to arrange itself, Mags called the formation for their squadron. She was easily able to relay the order, but getting into position with the others would have been a challenge. However, before she could move, her squadmates formed up around *her*, getting the group into perfect position without Mags having to do a thing. She was filled with a sense of gratefulness, as it meant she didn't have to remember the exact formations. Instead, she could focus on keeping track of the radar and other mission parameters.

Their squadron had been allocated one of the rear positions in a tactical support role. She assumed it was because they had the least training in both simulated and real combat.

The lead squadron reported on their group channel. *"Enemy contacts, full spread bearing three-zero-zero to zero-three-zero. Ten thousand to twenty thousand, three hundred knots closure."*

As Mags peered in the direction called, she knew there

was no point in reporting numbers. The Hunduns had gathered in one giant, swarming mass. The fleet commander ordered them into a full attack formation, and the forward armada fanned out so they would have a clear firing line. Her squadron was still assigned to the flanking position; their role would be more for support and reinforcements. Mags checked her ordinance; she was fully loaded with four long range AIM-500 and three AIM-320's.

As they drew closer to the Hun, her radar pinged the enemy targets. A sea of red filled her display, and compared to the tiny blue dots around her, they looked completely overwhelmed.

"Weapons hot, full attack! Limit comms," General Li called.

It was time.

Mags unlocked her weapons for the first time ever and targeted one group with her AIM-500. Even though they were one of the support squadrons, their long range was still enough to reach the hive of Hun ahead.

The sea of red rippled and started to scatter. Distinct groups of Hun formed their own mini-squadrons and approached their armada. She and her squadron emptied the last of their long-range weaponry and prepared for the next phase of the fight.

For the next few minutes, she kept careful watch on her radar contacts. It was difficult to focus on any single engagement, but from a top-down view, it didn't look good. Most squadrons were reporting 'weapons empty'.

The commander called for the reinforcements; they

needed to join the fight. As they approached the main battle, the chaos became evident. The armada was making headway, mostly in melee combat. Mags' squadron sent a volley of medium range missiles at some of the Hun not engaged with Fenixes.

Just as she was about to release her last missile, a warning sounded in her head.

ERROR: Missile jammed!

Mags' stomach dropped and her head spun. She felt the missile jammed in her tract, almost like she would feel food lodged in her throat if she didn't chew properly.

If the warhead detonated whilst still inside the launcher, she and the Fenix would be destroyed.

"I'm disengaging, I've got a jam!" She broke formation immediately, ignored the concerned radio calls from her team, and forced herself to focus.

If it detonated whilst they were still close together, it would obliterate her team.

She began following the emergency checklist, and after what seemed like an eternity deactivated the warhead. Unfortunately, the launcher was still disabled. The only way she could use the missile was if she tore it out of the tract and threw it at something.

In the panic of the jam, she hadn't been paying attention to the direction she'd been flying. Her flight path had taken her closer to where the Hun were congregating, though, luckily, the entire hive was engaged with the armada.

Just as she was about to turn back to join her squad, she saw it.

A huge target appeared at the edge of her radar limit; it must have been the size of a hundred Hun. She recycled her radar systems just to be sure, but when they came back online, it was still there. It hovered at such a low altitude, any lower and her radar would have assumed it was part of the terrain. Since it was still too far to get a visual, she highlighted her other sensors to confirm the readings. Her Lidar gave her a reading of an obscenely large mass, the infrared picking up a massive heat signature despite the distance from her, and, curiously, the environmental sensors were detecting a massive spike in toxic air around the mass.

There had always been rumours of a Hundun mothership, but nobody had seen it before. Before Mags could get closer to confirm her suspicions, it disappeared, the reading replaced with a hundred more targets that flickered to life on the screen. Mags tracked their movement as they rose from the surface of Earth. She tried to find the mothership again, but it was gone.

Mags swore to herself as a hundred more Hunduns were headed their way, fast.

She flipped and turned back toward her squadron. *"Targets incoming! Multiple spread!"*

"Oh, crap!" called Cliff.

Ash gasped through comms. *"Where did they come from?"*

"All squadrons. Formation Stone Wall!" General Li called. It was a defensive line that meant only one thing.

A final stand.

There was no possible way the remaining forces could

defeat so many. There was nowhere to go, the Huns would destroy them and leave everyone on the Worldship Honour to die. It would be the end for all humanity.

The enemy was hot on her tail as she screamed through the air. Ash from a nearby volcano filled the sky and made it difficult to see. Her eyes watered and her lungs burned. Mags considered climbing to a higher altitude, but then a thought occurred to her.

Instead of ascending, she started a downward dive, the change in direction allowed her to pick up her pace as she shot toward the ground.

"Get back into formation!" Shale called.

"I have an idea! Just stay with the others," she called back.

As the ash worked its way through the Fenix's system, Mags felt her head swim as she started to cough uncontrollably.

A couple of Hun had broken away from the main group and were chasing her down. They tried intercepting her flight path, and she employed the same strategy as she did in training, avoiding their clumsy attempts to grapple her. After she dodged the last one, she beat her wings several more times before pulling them back into a streamlined position. The rest of the hive passed overhead, ignoring or oblivious to the plight of a single doomed Fenix.

Mags knew this was her last chance.

Through the noxious grey cloud, she finally spied what she had been waiting for. The glowing haze of the volcano's mouth. The searing heat burned at the edges of her wings and threatened to shorten the critical electrical circuits keeping the neural link connected. Emergency warnings flared in her vision, every 'CRITICAL CAUTION' alarm blinking rapidly—airspeed, temperature, pressure... everything was redlining. She diverted all power to the neural link, disabling every other system. The HUD went blank, and the warning system went silent.

She didn't need them anymore.

With one winged arm, she reached for the last missile jammed in the launcher. It took a cry of determination and a desperate twist to yank it free, causing a leak of coolant from an adjacent chamber that dripped from her fuselage and sizzled into steam below her. She was only a thousand feet from the crater. Ignoring the pain flaring in her body and levelling out, she activated the warhead manually, and relief poured through her as it came to life.

She threw the launcher and missile directly into the middle of the volcano as she swopped overhead, then beat her wings with all her might to try and clear the vent before the inevitable explosion. A few seconds later, a deafening roar sounded behind her, and she felt the rush of violently hot air that preceded the inferno of the explosion.

The realisation that she would never see Willow or her family again was the last thing she thought about as her world turned black.

CHAPTER

THIRTEEN

"B*ut... he—*"

"She!"

"She's gonna be okay, right?"

"She should be. Talon unplugged her in time."

"What happens when the General finds out?"

"He won't find out."

"But you have to tell him, don't you? That Marsh—"

"Magnolia."

"Sorry, Magnolia is a woman."

The voices swirled around Mags. Her head was pounding, and she was too busy wishing she could claw her way back to quiet, blessed unconsciousness to care about what they were saying. At least, until she heard...

"Actually, she prefers Mags."

Eyes snapping open, Mags groaned as her retinas burned at the sudden brightness around her. She blinked away the pain and disorientation as five silhouettes hovered above her. Each one was familiar in its own way, but it was the one with the long hair that drew her attention.

"W-Willow?" she croaked. She rubbed her eyes and the shadows shifted, allowing her to see blurry, coloured shapes. Then reality dawned on her as she recognised Talon. "Oh, crap."

Talon straightened up, crossing his arms over his chest and glaring down his well-shaped nose at her. Beside him, Shale, Cliff, and Ash watched her warily.

"You're a woman," Talon said, tone clipped.

Mags glanced down and noticed the bandage wrapped around her torso and the fact she was covered in a sheet, not clothing. She blinked as she looked around, realising she was in Willow's room. In Willow's *bed*. Not only that, but Willow, Talon, and the rest of Moon Squadron were staring down at her.

Willow sighed. "We've been through this, Talon. She only did it to save her father."

Talon narrowed his eyes at her. "Oh? And do you think your father would be happy if I told him you were involved in this?"

"She's not involved in this. It was my decision and mine alone," Mags claimed without hesitation, voice feeling scratchy as she spoke. Talon simply raised an eyebrow at her. "Please, Talon... you have to understand. I just wanted to help. I know what the rules are. Frankly, I think they are—"

Mags would have kept rambling if Talon hadn't held up a hand and said, "We need to get back. I order the three of you never to speak of this to anyone. Marsh—Magnolia—

saved your lives out there. For that, I will keep this secret for her."

The worry that had been growing into a messy, tangled ball in Mags' stomach paused. It still rumbled and growled, but it was no longer gnawing at her. "Talon, thank you."

"Don't thank me," Talon snapped, shaking his head. "You made a fool out of myself and your—and the Moon Squadron, and you brought dishonour to your family. Luckily, your stunt with the volcano killed many of the Huns, and the armada was able to finish off the rest. Our people will survive."

Mags blinked. They defeated the Huns?

"Even the Mothership?" Mags blurted, twitching as she thought of that giant blip on her radar.

Talon narrowed his eyes at her. "What? There was no mothership."

"Yes, it was a huge mass on my screen before the final—"

"It was the final wave," Talon barked, cutting her off. He glanced at Willow and pointed his finger at Mags. "She stays here. Out of trouble. If you don't make sure of it, you can bet I will be telling your brother about your part in this." Talon rounded on the boys. "Move it, men! We have to get to the announcement of the *Honour's* return to Earth before someone notices we're missing."

"No!" Mags insisted. "I know what I saw, Talon. It was huge!"

Mags sounded frantic now. Even she could hear it. She

tried to sit up, but Willow sank onto the bed beside her and pressed a hand on her shoulder, keeping her down.

"Mags, please, you've been through a lot. Talon managed to pull you out of the flight capsule before it did any real damage, but—"

"You don't understand." Mags shook her aching head, frustration tearing at every part of her. "The mothership is down there, waiting for us to return. It will destroy the *Honour* before it can even get close to touching down. If I don't get out there, they will die. *We* will die."

Talon eyed her with suspicion. "Maybe you were seeing things. You did just dive into an active volcano to blow it up. Your Fenix is unsalvageable at this point. I'd be willing to bet your sensors were giving you false readings."

"No! I saw it before I dived into the volcano. I confirmed it with LIDAR and infrared too. You have to believe me!"

Talon looked up at the others. Cliff and Shale shrugged, but Ash squinted his eyes in thought.

"Wait, if you saw it before your bird crashed, then the telemetry would have been recorded in the black box," Ash said, sounding excited.

"Her bird is still in the infirmary, it was nearly dead when we found it. As far as I could tell, most of the avionics were fried," Shale explained.

The thought of her friends using their Fenix's claws to grip onto her own and bring it back to the Honour caused a surprising surge of emotion in Mags.

Cliff rolled his eyes. "It's the black box, you moron, it's

supposed to survive any crash. Even a kamikaze one like hers."

Drumming his fingers on the head of the bed, Talon said, "As far as I remember, it can take days to get the data from those things. There's a lot of security around the system."

"Leave that to me!" Willow chimed in with a mischievous grin. "If you can get me the box, I'll get the data."

Talon glanced at Mags. "Are you sure about this mothership? I could get into a lot of trouble giving the black box to a civilian."

Mags nodded. "I'm sure they'll forgive you if it means we don't all die."

After a few tense, drawn out moments of hesitation, Talon straightened and nodded. "Alright. Let's do this. Moon Squadron, with me." He looked at Mags. "You get some rest. We'll be back soon."

They left Mags and Willow alone together, and as soon as the door closed behind the boys, Willow sank down on the edge of the bed and reached up, brushing her fingertips over Mags' cheeks.

"I was so worried about you," she whispered.

Mags covered Willow's hand and leaned into it, letting out a soft sigh of relief at her touch. "How did they find you?" she asked.

"The tall one–"

"Ash?"

"Yeah, Ash. He saw me when we were dancing together at Tian, and I guess my face looked familiar to him. Then he remembered the article in the news about when Talon, my brother, and their squadron were interviewed after the mission that got Talon injured. All of the families were asked to pose for the photo, too... so he recognised me from that," Willow explained, not moving her hand away from Mags'. "It wasn't hard for them to find me then. Talon has been over here often enough that he knew where to bring you."

Mags blinked. Of course Ash had figured it out.

"They... they know about us," she whispered, worry making her hand tense.

Willow's cheeks flushed. "I suppose they do... but I think it is the least of their concerns at the moment."

"If they tell someone–"

"Shh..." Willow leaned in and silenced her concerns with a kiss. "You can't worry about that now. You need to rest."

"Rest?" Mags tried to sit up, but her entire body protested. "I can't rest, Willow. I need to get out there, I need to—"

"You need to rest," Willow repeated, far more firmly this time. She reached out, tugging Mags' pillow out from under her and resting it back against the headboard. Willow moved so that she was seated where Mags' pillow had been a moment before, and guided Mags to relax her head into her lap.

The way Willow started stroking Mags' scalp made every bit of fight drain from her.

"I've given you some of the medicine Talon stole from an emergency medkit. It will take a while to repair your injuries. The others are retrieving the black box. The best thing you can do for all of us is rest," Willow told her gently.

For once, Mags didn't argue. She just took Willow's free hand and pulled her arm over her chest, hugging it tight as she closed her eyes and let herself enjoy the tender ministrations of her girlfriend.

By the time the Moon Squadron returned, Mags had mostly recovered from her injuries. Despite her stunt, whether it was pure stubbornness or luck, the injuries transferred from the Fenix to her were only equivalent to first degree burns and smoke inhalation.

"We got it!" Ash announced as they burst through the door, holding the black box device over his head like some sort of trophy.

"Yeah, and I think Cliff made a new friend in the process." Shale winked.

Cliff grunted but his face was flushed with embarrassment.

"Can we concentrate on the issue at hand?" Talon suggested, glaring at the boys even though the corners of his lips flickered up for the barest of moments.

"Perfect, bring it here." Willow carefully slid out from under Mags, putting the pillow back under her head. She then walked over to the desk in the room, collecting the black box from Ash on the way, and plugged the device into her slate before she began typing away at the keyboard.

"How long is this going to take?" Talon asked, glancing back over his shoulder at the door to Willow's bedroom.

"Not long," Willow promised.

"Then why does it take days if we go through the right channels?" Ash asked, frowning at Willow, suspicion in his eyes.

Mags chuckled, her voice still feeling a little raw. "Bureaucracy."

Cliff raised an eyebrow at her. "Really? You're going to tell me that the only reason it takes so long is because of a little paperwork—"

"Okay, I'm in," Willow announced.

The Moon Squadron looked at her, dumbfounded.

"Told you she was clever." Mags winked at the boys, who all smirked back at her reference to the conversation they'd had in their quarters many nights ago.

Willow ignored the banter. "The security they use is much the same as every other part of the ship," she explained. "Please don't think that the speed means it was an easy hack. Let's just say I have a lot of practice."

Mags was tempted to warn Willow against sharing all of their secrets, but, to be fair, a little bit of extracurricular hacking was the least of their crimes at this point.

Talon pinched the bridge of his nose. "As your brother's best friend, I hope you appreciate the terrible situation you are dragging me into," he muttered, shaking his head.

With a winning smile, Willow forged on, "Anyway. I have the telemetry. Wow... you all need to look at this."

They all crowded around the screen. Willow made sure Mags could see it from her bed.

Eyes widening, Talon said, "It can't be!"

Cliff gasped. "Impossible!"

"Impossible? More like impressive!" Ash leaned in closer, his eyes reflecting the lines of code on the screen.

Mags sat up as she read from across the room. "Look at those readings! According to them, that creature is generating the toxins in the atmosphere. We thought was the individual Hunduns themselves changing the planet, but it was a mothership all along!"

"So, even after killing thousands of those things, this massive one is still down there? And it is the thing destroying Earth's atmosphere?" As Talon spoke, it was clear he was still stunned as he tried to wrap his head around the situation.

"It lured us down there; it knew we would send everything. We walked right into a trap." Cliff shook his head as he took a step back and crossed his arms over his chest.

"Yeah, and if Mags hadn't blown up a volcano, we'd all be goners by now," Shale added.

All eyes in the room turned to Mags. "Dumb luck, I guess?"

Silence fell between them as the group considered what their discovery meant not only for them but for the people of the *Honour*.

Finally, Ash broke the quiet with the question that was on everyone's minds. "What are we going to do?"

"We have to kill it," Talon said, his voice firm, as if he had already made the decision. "If we land the *Honour* on Earth now, it doesn't have enough fuel to take off again.

That thing will ambush us, and humanity will be as good as lost."

"Not only that, but it's also still poisoning the atmosphere. Even if it doesn't attack, we can't live down there," Willow pointed out, gesturing at the air quality readings on the screen.

"How are we going to kill it? Most of our Fenixes are out of commission. We used up all of our munitions," Ash muttered, his voice wavering with anxiety.

"I'm pretty sure we're out of volcanoes, too." Despite the morbidness of Shale's comment, Mags and the others laughed. It was a good way to ease the tension that was growing taut in the room.

The reprieve gave the group time to think, and after a few moments, Talon scratched his jaw and said, "We have a reserve fleet, older models with older systems. I think we can get into them. My father should be able to help us." Then, seeming to steel himself, he turned toward the door. "Moon Squadron, follow me."

Mags slid off the bed and looked around, finding her flight suit draped over the back of Willow's chair. She started to pull it on over her tights and bandaged torso.

"Hey, where are you going?" Willow rushed over to her.

"I have to get out there. You heard them, Willow. This is it."

"Are you crazy? You've done enough already, you saved everyone. It's time you took a break," Willow pleaded. Mags looked into her eyes as she reached up, pushing a strand of hair behind her ear.

"I need to do this."

After three seconds of stoic stubbornness, Willow's posture sagged as all the fight left her. "Fine, but I'm coming with you."

That, Mags thought, was a compromise she was happy to make.

FOURTEEN

Almost everyone on the ship had gathered in the main meeting hall for the announcement of the Hundun's defeat and the Worldship Honour's return to Earth.

Mags and Willow filtered in after Talon, who was slowly weaving his way through the crowd. At the front of the cavernous hall, General Li stood off to the side of the dais the emperor was on whilst he delivered his address. The general didn't seem to spot the group until they were just metres away from his location, but when he did, his eyes widened and his face set with anger. He fixed Talon with a withering glare, but Talon didn't falter.

Before the Moon Squadron reached the edge of the stage, General Li stepped away. He strode over to them and snatched Talon's injured arm in a hard grip, dragging him to the side of the hall. Mags, Willow, and the others followed along.

"What are you doing here? I told you that you and your

squadron are confined to quarters until we can arrange disciplinary action for the dishonour you have brought upon the fleet," General Li hissed, looking over his shoulder to make sure he wasn't overheard as he scolded his son. Then, his gaze snagged on Mags, and his expression soured with repulsion.

"Please, General," Talon said, bowing his head and keeping his voice calm and even, "One of my pilots discovered something on Earth. We looked at the black box telemetry—"

"You did what?" If they had been somewhere more private, Mags had no doubt General Li's whisper would have been a roar.

"There is a mothership still on—"

General Li raised a hand right up to Talon's face.

"Do not come to me with rumours and myths, son! How dare you?" General Li spat, his back stiffening as a few of the people nearby turned to watch the unfolding drama. "Leave now, or I will bypass the punishment and have you all court-martialled instead."

Talon's expression turned stony, and there was a tic in his jaw that made Mags wonder how hard it was for him to restrain himself in that moment. Either way, he seemed to take a slow breath before saluting the General.

"Apologies for the interruption then, General Li. My squadron and I will return to my quarters to await punishment," he said. Then, to Mags' absolute horror, he turned on his heel and walked out.

Mags, Willow, and the boys had no other option but to scramble after him.

When they all got out to the hall, Mags blurted, "We can't just walk away!"

Talon stopped and turned to face her. "Of course we can't," he said, sounding annoyed that she had thought he intended to. "If my father will not help you get into the reserve fleet hangar, I will."

Talon didn't waste any time leading the Moon Squadron to the hangar that housed the reserve fleet of older Fenix models. It was empty and unguarded, probably because everyone was expected to be at the emperor's victory announcement. He walked the group right up to a set of pods at the back corner of the hangar and ordered them to buckle in. He turned to Willow, who stood by, watching nervously. "You hacked into the system to change Magnolia's details, correct?"

Willow nodded sheepishly.

"Can you hack in again?"

"I've been hacking in for as long as I remember," she confessed.

"Good. Get in there. Lock the hangar doors. Make sure no one gets in here," Talon told her. He pulled the sling off his arm. "Guess the doctor's orders won't matter if I'm dead." He moved over to a pod of his own.

"I'm going to broadcast your mission, too," Willow called out, walking over to a nearby wall console.

Mags blinked at her. "We're going to get into enough trouble as it is. That will just give them more evidence."

Willow grinned. "If the whole ship is watching you save our lives for real, there is no way they will be able to punish you for it. The people won't stand for it."

That was one thing Mags loved about Willow. She was such an optimist. As much as she disagreed, they didn't have time to argue. She had to trust her friend, just as Willow had trusted her. So, instead of arguing, she gave her one last smile before slipping into her own pod and connecting to the neural link.

Due to their covert operation, there was no point in getting clearance for departure. They slipped out of the hanger unnoticed and used well known radar blind spots to avoid being detected.

It was only a matter of minutes before Mags was once again feeling the burn of entry into Earth's atmosphere. It felt hotter than she remembered, and she wasn't sure if that was because of her own healing burns or because the Fenix she was in was an older model. That thought made her realise that she didn't know as much about the ship she was flying as she would have liked. *"Are we fully loaded?"* she asked, hoping Talon would know more than she did.

"Each bird has a full compliment. They are using older generation avionics and weapon systems, but it will have to do," Talon replied. *"As for the mission, make your calls. You're running point on this, as you have had eyes on the mothership before."*

"Copy that." Mags scanned the sky ahead, getting her bearings and setting up her nav coordinates to lead her

back to the location where she saw the mothership blip. *"Silent Dragon, Gold Twenty."*

"Two contacts, five-zero-zero miles bearing three-two-zero, flight level one-two-zero," Shale called.

"Copy." Mags sighted the two enemy targets on her radar guidance display. Judging by their speed and height, they looked to be scouts. Her concerns that they had not, in fact, wiped out the Hundun army was now confirmed. She wondered if more had been hiding beneath the ground, or the cover of their mothership.

They could either engage and take them out quickly or investigate to see if they were alone.

Mags opted to investigate.

"Three more contacts, six-zero-zero miles, bearing zero-niner zero, flight level two-zero-zero. Looks like a split squadron. Should we engage?" Ash called.

"Negative. They're spotters. We need to descend and find the mothership," Mags replied, a picture of the flight field forming in her mind.

They dropped below the remaining ash cloud formed from the previous eruption. She could taste the sulphur, but it wasn't as thick as it had been before, and her ship's filters handled it easily enough.

Mags saw the mothership with her own eyes before it pinged on her radar. The massive shape hovered just above the ground. It even visually matched the ground; the murky brown hide and ribbed carapace looking like barren, rolling hills. A constant stream of thick, noxious clouds puffed from the cracks in the creature's hide. Mags wasn't surprised they had missed it. It did an excellent job of masking itself as terrain.

Just as Mags was about to tell the others she saw it, forty new Hunduns shot out from the creature's belly, hurtling toward them. Just like their training scenarios, they were outnumbered and definitely outgunned; their older weaponry wouldn't have nearly the same yield as their other Fenixes. Every shot had to count.

"Weapons free, engage targets. Formation Distant Dragon, Fire Twenty!"

The others formed up around her as she locked her first target. She released her long-range missile, and the rest fired after her. Mags watched on her radar as all five of their missiles met their marks. Their enemy had no time to react, but the hits were far enough apart that the collateral was minimal.

"They certainly know we're here now," Talon muttered.

Mags scanned the sky around her as the swarm of Huns grew closer. She fired another shot at one of the clusters before turning around and retreating. The rest of Moon Squadron did the same. The Hun didn't have missiles that could track targets like they did, but they did fire hypersonic spines from their claws that travelled just as fast, sometimes faster. As if on cue, she spied a flurry of them headed straight toward her, but they were far enough away it was easy to evade them. She checked her radar contacts again and called for another round of weapons fire from her group.

There were two whoops of celebration before Cliff grunted, *"No joy."*

Mags let out a slow breath. So, Cliff missed one shot. That was okay, they had gotten another eight down. She continued calling formations.

Their squadron split in two, with Mags and Ash taking the lower altitude, while Cliff, Shale, and Talon took the higher. By splitting up like they did, it was less likely they would be surrounded. The enemy squadrons reformed to give chase. They were still outnumbered, but thankfully, Mags had a plan.

"Pouncing Snake. Fire Twelve!" Mags reared her craft in midair, banking and flipping. Her stomach rolled, but the timing was perfect, as she managed to avoid another volley of spines.

"Fox Two!" Mags sent a missile in front of the pursuing mass. She heard the others call the same, and the enemy contacts on her radar disappeared en masse. As part of the formation tactic, she let loose another two missiles at the remaining fighters. After they had exhausted the last projectiles, there were only a few blips of red left on her radar.

"Three contacts, bearing three-four-five, four-zero miles, eight thousand. They're turning and running," Cliff reported.

"Hunting Lion, Neutral. Finish them off with the rail guns," she ordered, knowing they'd all run out of missiles. The air around them rattled with the pounding of high-speed bolts flying through the air. Her entire body shook with the vibrations of the powerful ammunition release.

Ash laughed over comms. *"This is a piece of cak—"*

The sudden cut alarmed Mags, and she whipped around to see what happened. From the corner of her eye, she spied four Hun screaming toward them. One of them had already crashed into Ash, the wing clipping off and taking part of his tail with it.

Mags flipped over to prepare herself, but their previous formation wasn't designed to defend against a rear attack. Cliff and Shale attempted to evade but were too late. A pair of Huns crashed into them. She lost track of Talon.

The only reason Mags narrowly avoided her target was because she was the lead craft. She managed to release a volley of bolts at the Hun before it got within slashing distance. Some of her shots landed, which gave her the upper hand in the melee. After several tumbling turns in the air, she managed to claw her way to victory as her opponent plummeted toward the ground. She glanced around to take stock of the remainder of her squadron.

It wasn't going well; they were below her now and falling rapidly, their older Fenixes didn't have the enhanced strength and armour of the newer models, they had to rely on natural strength and skill to fight now. There was no more chatter on the radio, only grunts of pain and struggle. She assessed the situation and noted that Cliff had somehow managed to break free of the grapple of two Hunduns. They thrashed wildly at him, but he seemed calm and controlled. As one dove toward him, he managed to position it in a clawhold. Shale was holding his own from what she could see, getting his opponent into a shoulder claw. Ash, on the other hand, was struggling the most. His enemy had him in a lock and was pushing him toward the ground.

"Ash, I'm coming."

"No! We've got this, take out the mothership!" Talon called. Her eyes widened as she saw him screaming in from above, crash-tackling the Hun engaged with Ash and pulling it into a steep dive. He managed to wrench it off Ash and wrestle it into the dreaded mandible claw.

Mags reared her Fenix back around. Their skirmish had taken them away from the mothership, and she could see it retreating further into the distance. Luckily for her, it was slow and lacked any kind of manoeuvrability.

Mags only had a few hundred rounds in her rail gun left. She needed to make every shot count. With her initial volley, she pelted the side of the creature, causing it to shake and growl in anger. It turned its head toward her as it pushed off the ground, its giant maw opening to reveal a set of razor-sharp, glistening teeth larger than Mags' ship. She dove beneath it just as it snapped its jaws shut with a sonorous boom, flying in the small space between the ground and the beast's underbelly and gawking up at the massive behemoth.

In the centre of the mothership's torso was a faint glowing pulse. It thrummed at an even pace, suffusing the area around her with a subtle glow. It was covered in a thick, gelatinous flesh that was far more tender looking than its hardened carapace. This was its vulnerable spot. She had to attack while she could. She let the remaining rounds of her rail guns loose. The ammunition pierced through the soft skin, and blood and gore spurted outward.

The creature pulled away from the ground. It attempted to curl up to protect itself, but Mags didn't let it.

She may not have had any ammunition left, but her Fenix itself was a weapon.

With the absolute certain knowledge that she had to protect humanity, Mags urged her Fenix forward. She cried out as the nose of her ship slammed into the glowing core of the mothership. Then she clawed and slashed as deep as she could, tearing through layer after layer of flesh and organs.

Her Fenix burrowed its way deeper and deeper until she came to the source of the glow, but just as she was about to strike into the heart of the beast, she felt a large, clawed hand encompass her entire body. It gripped her so tightly it squeezed the breath from her. The injuries she received from her previous stunt came back in full force as her Fenix was crushed under immense pressure. Darkness clawed at the edges of her vision, and just as she was sure she was going to die, the death-grip around her fuselage loosened, and she spiralled toward ground.

As her vision cleared, she looked up to see that the mothership was thrashing at several flying targets diving around her.

Moon Squadron had survived.

Talon wrestled with the claw that recently grabbed her, whilst Cliff dove around the other. In single combat they were no match for the gargantuan beast. It was bigger and stronger in every aspect, but every time the mothership grappled one of them in her massive claws, another would dive in to distract it by attacking another part of it. Their tag teaming technique was synced perfectly, and Talon was coordinating their strikes, even Ash with his injured tail still managed to keep its attention by latching onto its head.

The creature roared in pain and anger, its cry piercing her ears. The cacophony was followed shortly by a terrifying reply in the mist. At this altitude, her older generation avionics couldn't distinguish anything, but judging by the mass of shadows arising from the ground, she knew what was coming. The mothership's brood was joining the fight.

"It's now or never, finish it off!" Talon ordered, voice strained. He must have seen the incoming wave.

Everything had led to this moment.

Magnolia thought of the people on the Worldship Honour, her squadron, her family... and Willow.

She was fighting for them all of them.

She couldn't fail now.

Mags focused her mind. The fight in front of her and the incoming danger faded away. Control and balance was all that remained. Everything around her slowed down as if moving in slow motion.

With one final breath, she tucked her wings in tight and catapulted toward the exposed heart. Mags crashed into the creature headfirst with all the force she could muster. She felt resistance against her body, and everything inside was dark, but this time she allowed nothing to slow her crawl as she fought through the flesh, through the burning heat of the heart, and—

She burst out the other side.

Blood and gore sprayed in a macabre fountain around her as she unfurled her wings and soared into the sky. She turned back to watch as the mothership went limp. The remaining Hun suddenly dropped from the sky, falling to the ground en masse. The behemoth hit the ground, a cloud of brown dirt ballooning around it, and a deep rumble vibrating through the air.

As the dust settled around them, the Moon Squadron fell into a deep silence. Mags blinked as the world around them fell still.

Peaceful.

"We did it."

Relief flooded through her, and her body, and consequently the Fenix, shook with relief. She flew past the corpse of the mothership and descended lower and lower. No new blips appeared on her screen. No new enemies came flying at them. Tentatively, Mags settled her ship down on the soil of earth. She felt the dirt and patchy grass crunch beneath the landing gear of her Fenix, and her eyes burned with emotion.

"We freaking did it!" The reverent, awe-filled moment was shattered as Cliff, Shale, and Ash crashed into the ground all around her. Mags wasn't sure who had screamed out and broken the quiet, but she didn't care. *They had won!*

"I hate to break up the party, but we're going to have a lot to answer for when we get back to the Honour. We need to move out." Talon flew over their heads, dipping his left wing in a gesture of a flying salute. *"We'll be back down here to play in the dirt soon enough. At least... if the emperor is in a benevolent mood."*

CHAPTER

FIFTEEN

It was with great relief that Mags and the Moon Squadron discovered that the emperor *was* in a good mood.

General Li, however, was not.

The five of them were in the meeting hall, the remaining population of the *Honour* at their backs, as they stood before the two most powerful people on the ship. Each of them was sporting an assortment of bandages over their new wounds, but they stood with their backs straight and chins held high. After returning their Fenixes to the hangar and disengaging from the flight pods, Willow had released the locks holding the doors closed, and they were quickly apprehended by security.

When they first appeared in the hall, it was to a rousing cheer of support from those gathered. As they looked up and around, all of the screens were showing replays of their exploits down on Earth. Mags had never been more grateful for the cleverness of her best friend. She had tried to look around to find her, but there were too many people, and they had been rushed to the front without a chance to gawk about.

"I cannot believe you would be so irresponsible," General Li growled, standing over his son and glaring down at him, the quiet rage simmering off him. "Stealing five Fenixes and leading a crew of four inexperienced young men—"

Li's eyes slid to Mags, and he frowned.

"Three young men and one *woman*," the emperor corrected, stepping forward. General Li pressed his lips together and bowed his head. "You led a crew of three inexperienced young men and one woman back to Earth, without permission. What do you have to say for yourself, Captain Li?"

Talon raised his chin, ignoring the way his father was glaring for him. "The disobedience and theft were my responsibility. However, the intelligence came from Magnolia. Without her, the mothership would have survived, and we would have had to fight them again. Not only that, but we would never have known the mothership was the source of the toxic gas. I apologise for our insubordination and will take whatever punishment you must deliver on behalf of myself and my entire squadron. They were just following orders." Then, he bowed his head.

Mags' eyes widened at his offer to take the punishment for all of them. That could have him in prison for the rest of his life. She looked over at him, ready to protest, but the emperor spoke.

"Luckily for you, Captain Li, I admire the bravery and

conviction with which you all conducted yourselves, if not the methods." Then, he turned to Magnolia. "And you, child, are a surprise indeed. By all accounts, you not only defeated the mothership in your rogue mission, but you also risked your own life to cull the Hundun to end the first battle."

A hot blush crept over Mags' cheeks at the clear surprise in the emperor's tone. As much as she appreciated his acceptance of what she had done, a bitter part of her wondered if he would have seemed as shocked if a man had been the one to do it. Instead of pointing that out, she just said, "Thank you, your Imperial Highness."

"As a reward for your skill, I wish to bestow the honour of a favourable marriage upon you and your family. Simply name a match from your cohort, and you can consider the marriage arranged. And, to celebrate your heroism, you shall be the first couple wed on Earth." The emperor's proclamation earned a cheer from the crowd. He really knew what to say to get them on his side. He gestured out to those gathered. "What do you say, Magnolia? Who will be lucky enough to take the Champion of the Honour's hand in marriage?"

Mags' heart skipped a beat. She thought back over the emperor's wording and smiled to herself as an idea formed in her head. Biting her lip, she glanced over at Willow.

Her best friend's dark eyes were wavering with a sheen of tears at this news. At the possibility that their romance would be cut short. As Mags' smile widened, so did Willow's eyes. Understanding dawned in them, and her pretty, bow shaped lips parted as Mags returned her attention to the emperor.

"Thank you for the honour, your Imperial Highness. I gratefully accept your permission to choose my own match from my birth cohort. As such, I would like to announce the name of the person I will wed," Mags said, raising her voice for all to hear. A cheer rippled through the group. For a ship where life had been so monotonous for so many years, this was turning out to be a rather exciting day.

The emperor chuckled at the theatrics and swept his hand toward the crowd once more. "Please, my dear, do not keep us in suspense." He glanced at the three boys standing on the dais between Mags and Talon. His lips twitched with amusement, most likely assuming she would pick one of them. The boys seemed to think it, too, as they stood a little taller and puffed their chests out.

Gross, Mags thought to herself.

Instead, she walked along the edge of the dais until she stood before Willow. Well, she stood for only so long as to ensure everyone was watching, before she dropped to her knee and took Willow's hand. She cleared her throat and raised her voice. "Willow, will you do me the honour of becoming my wife?"

The crowd, which had previously been buzzing with anticipation, fell dead silent. There was a whoosh of rustling uniforms as everyone turned toward the emperor to gauge his reaction. He remained impossibly still, save for a twitch in his left eye.

The seconds felt like hours as Mags held Willow's soft, warm hand. Her heart was hammering against her ribs so loudly she could have sworn it would be audible back on Earth. She wondered in that moment if she had finally pushed *too* far. Instead of cowering, she turned back to meet the emperor's calculating stare.

What would happen if he rescinded his offer? He had made a public promise to reward her, after naming her the champion of their ship. Would they ever trust him again if he recanted his offer?

What would it cost to grant it to her?

Slowly returning his attention to the crowd, the emperor took in the sea of faces watching him. Waiting for an answer. "I believe the Champion has made her offer. What do you say, Willow?"

Mags' head spun. Her ears rang. She couldn't believe it.

She barely heard Willow's whispered, "Yes!" as the crowd roared their approval.

Then, nothing else mattered. The entire ship could have faded away around them and she wouldn't have noticed, because Willow's arms were around her, and their lips were pressed together.

Even though it was the sweetest kiss of her life, it ended far too soon when the Emperor called for the attention of the crowd.

Blushing, and realising that she had just given the entire population of the *Honour* quite the show, Mags gave Willow an apologetic smile and moved to stand beside her.

"People of the Worldship Honour, this has been a momentous day. With Earth saved, we are finally free to return to our ancestral home. It will not be an easy journey, but the fortitude and strength you have shown over the decades gives me hope that it will be possible," the emperor said, his voice ringing through the cavernous room. "We have some busy times ahead, so please... go home, spend time with your family, and cherish the quiet moment that the bravery of our people has earned us."

With that, the people at the back of the hall started to file out.

"Well... that was quite the show," Shale muttered as he, Cliff, Ash, and Talon came to stand beside Mags and Willow.

Ash elbowed him. "I believe you were supposed to say *congratulations.*"

"Don't mind Shale, he's just mad you didn't pick him," Cliff added.

Talon shook his head at their banter. "You did well today, Magnolia. It was an honour to fly with you. I hope you will remain with Moon Squadron when we return to Earth. We will need to keep flying to ensure the planet is secure."

Mags' eyes widened with excitement. She glanced at where the emperor and General Li were deep in conversation. "Can I do that?"

"Don't underestimate how powerful the emperor's favour is," Talon said with a wink. He patted her on the shoulder before turning to join the two men for their discussion.

"I'm looking forward to sleeping in my own bed again," Ash said, looking past their small group as the hall slowly emptied, clearly impatient to join the stream of people going home.

"I'm looking forward to my mother's dumplings." Cliff grinned.

Shale snorted. "I'm just keen to be able to shower in privacy."

That made Mags laugh. "Me too…"

The boys blinked at her for a few moments before everything fell into place.

"Oh! Well, now that all makes sense," Ash said, nodding in understanding.

Shale punched Mags' shoulder. "Are you trying to tell us you don't always stink that much?"

"Definitely not," Willow said, slipping her hand into Mags'. "She usually smells wonderful."

That made the boys shut their mouths.

Mags grinned at Willow and then let out a heavy sigh as she looked toward the door. Almost everyone had filed out, but as she took in the stragglers, she realised the only people left were her own family.

"I… I guess I need to face them," Magnolia said, the lightness of the situation dissipating.

Mags tried to let go of Willow's hand, but she held tight. "You don't need to do this—or anything else—alone."

A rush of affection warmed Mags, and she leaned in to kiss Willow's cheek. "Thank you."

Instead of trying to leave her behind, Mags tightened her hand around Willow's and led her over to where her family were waiting.

Mags' chest swelled with conflicting emotions as she focused on her father. She had not seen him since before she ran away. She knew he hadn't wanted her to interfere, and he had to be furious that she had not only been discovered for her deception, but taken such radical advantage with the emperor's favour.

Still clinging tight to Willow's hand, Magnolia cleared her throat. "Baba, I—"

Her father raised his hand. "Magnolia…"

The way he said her name held such exasperation.

"Please, I—"

"I am very proud of you," her father said, cutting off her attempt to give him reasons.

Mags froze at the unexpected words.

"You flew and fought in a way that brings our ancestors honour, and you have shown an integrity that so few people dare to wield," he continued. "Thank you for your duty, your love, and your bravery."

His face shone with his respect for her, and it took Mags' breath away.

Beside him, her mother beamed and her grandmother grinned. Reed was almost bouncing with excitement, but River's eyes widened in annoyance. Mags could just imagine he was wondering why she was being praised for her rebelliousness, when he was always in trouble for it.

Then, her father stepped forward, ahead of her family. He slowly lowered his top half in a bow that made Magnolia choke on her next breath.

She rushed forward, quickly pulling him to stand and throwing her arms around him.

Her father's posture was stiff at first, but when he

realised what she was doing, he relaxed and hugged her back.

One by one, her family members joined the embrace. They hugged, her mother sobbed, and River complained about not being able to breathe.

When the embrace ended, Mags' grandmother patted her on the head and leaned in close. "I've always liked Willow," she said with a wink.

Magnolia chuckled and looked back over her shoulder at where Willow was watching the reunion with tears welling in her eyes. A warm, contented smile curved Mags' lips at the sight of her friend—no, fiancé.

"Does that mean she can stay for dinner tonight?" Mags asked.

It was her grandmother's turn to chuckle. "Stay for dinner? Aiya, girl! She can stay forever!"

With that, she reached for Willow's hand again. It had been a long few weeks, but as Magnolia finally walked the familiar corridors back to her family's apartment, she realised she had everything that mattered with her right by her side.

ILLUSTRATIONS

BY CLAUDIO S

Willow cuts Magnolia's hair.

Page 26

Magnolia in combat training.

Page 44

Magnolia's Fenix bursts through the mothership.

Page 141

Magnolia kisses Willow.

Page 147

ABOUT "REAWAKENED"

"Reawakened" is a series of standalone retellings of myths, legends, classics, and more. It puts a new spin on old tales for modern Young Adult and New Adult audiences. The retellings will cover many different genres and styles, providing a set of stories as diverse as its readers.

For updates on what is coming next in the "Reawakened" series, visit www.livevans.com.au or follow Liv Evans (@LivEvansWrites) on Instagram, Tiktok, or Facebook.

If you enjoyed Magnolia (Reawakened), please consider leaving a review on one of the following sites: Goodreads or Amazon.

IF YOU ENJOYED THIS STORY...

If you enjoyed Magnolia (Reawakened) please consider leaving a review on one Goodreads or Amazon.

Reader reviews are crucial for helping indie authors share their stories with the world.

If you would like more news, updates, sneak peeks, and bonus content, visit www.livevans.com.au or follow Liv at @LivEvansWrites on Instagram, TikTok, and Facebook.

ALSO BY LIV EVANS

FOR NEW ADULT READERS:

The Derivates Rising Trilogy

1. The Underground

2. The Hub

3. Free Citizens

FOR ADULT READERS:

The Code of Us

By Liv Evans and Jay Thomas

The Triple C Reports

1. The Voidstalker Extraction